About the Author

From Newcastle, with Scottish origins, I have been living in the French Alps near Lake Annecy since my first job in a ski resort after university. Over the years, I have been a ski instructor, white-water rafter, estate agent, full-time mum to three sons, now grown, but these days I am an English teacher in a local high school. In this lovely area, I spend my free time skiing, walking in the mountains, swimming in the lake or gardening to the soundtrack of buzzards, woodpeckers and cuckoos.

As a European polyglot family, we love the resulting mishmash of cultures!

Best Dad Ever

Cathie Earle

Best Dad Ever

Olympia Publishers
London

www.olympiapublishers.com
OLYMPIA PAPERBACK EDITION

Copyright © Cathie Earle 2022

The right of Cathie Earle to be identified as author of this work has been asserted in accordance with sections 77 and 78 of the Copyright, Designs and Patents Act 1988.

All Rights Reserved

No reproduction, copy or transmission of this publication may be made without written permission.
No paragraph of this publication may be reproduced, copied or transmitted save with the written permission of the publisher, or in accordance with the provisions of the Copyright Act 1956 (as amended).

Any person who commits any unauthorised act in relation to this publication may be liable to criminal prosecution and civil claims for damage.

A CIP catalogue record for this title is available from the British Library.

ISBN: 978-1-80074-302-1

This is a work of fiction.
Names, characters, places and incidents originate from the writer's imagination. Any resemblance to actual persons, living or dead, is purely coincidental.

First Published in 2022

Olympia Publishers
Tallis House
2 Tallis Street
London
EC4Y 0AB

Printed in Great Britain

Chapter One

"Best dad ever!" He traced the letters with his fingers and sighed. Not any more. His battered old pencil case was nothing but a relic from the past.

"Fred, can you do Thursday night? Bernie has to take his kids to a meeting." There was an abrasive tone to the director's voice.

"Sure, no problem, he can get me back sometime." 'I still have kids you know…'

Sitting round this table still brought him out in a sweat. Now when he sat down to Monday morning team meetings, the memory of the most excruciatingly embarrassing moments of his life flashed in front of him. He was pretty sure it was in everybody else's minds too. From this very spot he had been obliged to confess to extra conjugal activity in front of all his colleagues, including the girl in question of course. And while mouths were still hanging open, he had been forced to admit that it was his son (at fourteen) who had hacked into his on-line work schedule. Theo had posted various cleverly photo-shopped, explicit suggestions of what he thought his father would be indulging in, who with, when and where, leaving his hurt and disarray in full public view on the school timetable of all places. Fred had discovered the truth the night before in a traumatic tearful scene, but it had been too late to postpone the meeting. The meeting had been called specially to try and ascertain where the electronic graffiti had been coming from.

He couldn't believe he had been so naïve, he had taught teenage boys all his life, he should have guessed. But then he had never done anything that needed hiding before, he had never learnt to cheat. He had been found out immediately and the consequences had been irrevocable.

A small hand stroked his thigh softly. He picked it up and put it back. She could feel his tension, but Emma just didn't understand the heart-break behind it. He just couldn't bear public displays of affection, here of all places. He could feel the judgement of his fellow workers and friends. Some of them were happily married and had been saddened and threatened by the situation. Some of his male contemporaries had obviously let their imaginations run wild while the women seemed united in their condemnation. His younger colleagues, both male and female, thought it odd and a little unsavoury.

He pulled his eyes back to the pencil case. It had been a Christmas present a couple of years ago. Theo had scratched the words into the soft leather with a compass, Lucie had coloured each letter with a different colour felt pen. They were a team, twenty months apart in age and really good friends. And now neither of them had spoken to him for four months and two days. He rubbed his forehead and heard the blessed words which signalled the end of the meeting. A class full of trouble-making kids would stop him thinking about his own worries for a while, as long as he could manage to ignore the occasional muttered slur about his sex life.

Emma was neatly finishing the last fold of her swan. This was the tricky part, gently pulling and distorting the paper without tearing it. But she was expert and the swan was hatched effortlessly. She lined it up with the two others she had already made. The meeting had been really dragging. She put her hand on Fred's thigh, but he brushed it off. God he was prudish. She looked up and saw that her legs were the focus of at least two of her male colleagues, opposite. It was an Indian summer and still warm enough for her favourite denim mini skirt. Her legs were horse-chestnut brown and her toenails shimmered with bronze nail varnish in her barely-there sandals. These old married men were so predictable. She could practically see their imaginations working. She ran her hands down the inside of her thighs, that would get them going. She caught a glare from a female colleague, one who couldn't seem to be bothered to even brush her hair in the morning let alone moisturise her thighs. Get over yourself, you old bag. Time to adjust to the idea, Fred is mine now. Why hadn't they got used to it yet? They weren't the only couple amongst the staff after all. She wanted them just to be a normal couple, albeit still in the honeymoon stage. If only Fred would put his arm around her occasionally or walk into school holding her hand. But he had told her that it would be unprofessional and so she still felt like a dirty little secret even though secret was the last thing their relationship was now.

She thought back to this time last year when she had first realised that the good-looking, charming, but apparently very married sports teacher was looking at her whenever he thought he wasn't being observed. She had caught his surreptitious glances once or twice. Of course, they had often exchanged the open friendly smiles which were his trademark, but those glances had shown a different type of interest. She had started to wear flirtier, shorter skirts for meetings knowing that from his position opposite her, her bare legs would be directly in view under the desks. She had offered to help with an after-school stretching class, his hands using her body to demonstrate positions, had been warm through her Lycra. As the weather warmed up there was less and less Lycra between his hands and her flesh, which she had kept immaculately smooth. Emma herself had never had a serious relationship, she had never seen the point in tying herself down, putting up with all those compromises, giving up on the thrill of a first kiss, suffering tedious domesticity. Both her parents were into their third marriages or equivalent, whether through sheer optimism or ineptitude she didn't know or even really care. But she was twenty-eight and the steadying kindness of Fred coupled with the electricity of his touch and the tension of weeks of undeclared interest had its effect on her. And of course, it was forbidden.

It was her first teaching post and she enjoyed it. It was an amazing place to work really, set in the middle of the Alps in a pretty market town near a beautiful lake. The students were training to work in the mountains and that meant that they had a day out walking, climbing or skiing every week. Emma had nearly finished her mountain leader qualification which meant she was one of the lucky members of staff who spent two days a week out on the hill. As the end of her first year had drawn near, the weather had been making the school zing with a hormonal buzz. The holidays were looming, she wouldn't see Fred for ages and quite frankly she had been dutiful for too long.

So she had organised a staff night out, a midsummer's night picnic on the beach with stand-up paddle by moonlight for those who wished. The rosé, the sunset, the beautiful still surface of the lake with the moon reflected in it as they cut silently through the warm water, followed by more rosé, had all combined. The result had been the kiss she had been dreaming of. One kiss had been enough to ignite the need which had been simmering for weeks. They had left the beach, Emma, sober enough to drive Fred, who wasn't, exactly where she wanted him.

Fred had kissed her and blamed the moonlight; he'd let himself be driven to a bed which was not his own and blamed the rosé. When he found his hand on the flesh which had been tantalisingly hidden by fragments of cloth up until then, he had nothing left to blame, but Emma had not given him a chance to have second thoughts. His brain flashed wife, guilt, but she had already eased herself down onto him. Rational thought fled. He was inside her, promise broken, he went with it.

Fred had surfaced the next morning in hell. He knew things had been strained at home. It was true that Margot was working harder than ever, seemed more interested in the kids than him, never had the energy to do anything even vaguely sporty which, it had to be said, was starting to show physically, but she was his partner in life and she would be desperately worried about him. As he ran his hand over his face and his fingers through his hair, the feeling of despair was replaced by another which he had all but forgotten. Emma knew, like all women of her generation, that the way to a man's heart was not through his mouth as previous generations had thought, but with hers. Swept away by sensations and Emma's infectious enthusiasm, Fred buried his conscience in a sexual headiness he hadn't felt in years. And he rose to the task, delighting in the dewy youthfulness of her skin, in the pink, soft nipples as yet unchewed by a hungry infant, and how she could bend. God.

He had come to his senses quite quickly and returned home. It would be a one-time mistake; he would never ever stray again. His heart was with his family and his wife, his home. He was, after all, a dedicated family man. But he had underestimated the effects on his body. Usually dampened by routine and kids, his libido had been released and wanted more. It felt more like a need than a want. That evening he made love to Margot, happy that it was the weekend and so it wasn't so unusual. The relief, but then he lost himself and he suddenly pushed her legs up round his neck in a way that made her squeal in protest and him snap out of his fantasy.

The next trial was the weekly Monday morning meeting. The seemingly innocent flirting which had made the meetings so pleasant over the last few weeks had been abruptly usurped by charged feelings of lustful guilt, and then panic, when he realised that for Emma, it wasn't over yet. He could see the promise in her eyes, and it was no longer imagination and fantasy, now he knew that the reality surpassed all that. One more time, sober and in control and then he would give it up forever, go back to his lovely, loving wife. But he would have to have one more time, to have her one more time. He groaned slightly and squirmed in his chair, his best friend looked at him quizzically, but fortunately a cross table argument distracted him and the moment was gone.

Emma, of course, had no such reticence. She had enjoyed herself, more than she had expected if she was honest. He had been so appreciative and hadn't been afraid of showing it and her repertoire was far from finished yet. She had a strong feeling that some of the things she had in mind had been off his menu for a while. She could make him feel so good and she loved that. She brushed her hand against her breast and crossed her legs, pressing her thighs together which made her skirt ride even higher. She couldn't wait too long for a repeat performance, maybe there would be an opportunity at lunchtime. She sighed under her breath, her neighbour turned to her.

"I know, it's so boring, isn't it?"

And so it had continued, Fred became more and more hooked on such athletic uninhibited sex, while Emma became more and more addicted to her sexual power over him. The risks became greater, the desire to touch each other became difficult to resist, their offices were not private, occasionally someone looked at them a little oddly, but it could all have died down if it hadn't been for Theo.

Fred still didn't know how Theo had found out about him and Emma, he hadn't been able to bring himself to ask him. He had thought he had been careful with his phone and that he had been normal and attentive at home. Somehow though, his son had known that he had been sleeping with someone other than his mother and even worse that it was with the pretty young workmate that Theo himself had the hots for. Even then he hadn't come and confronted his dad, instead he had photoshopped some photos from the school website and added them to the online timetable. Skilful, but acutely embarrassing. Fred had literally vomited into the waste-paper bin in his office when they came up on his screen. He had to go and see the boss, and the IT guy to get them taken down before the whole school saw them. He had gone home then and waited for Margot to get home. His face told her how bad things were before he even had to open his mouth. Somehow, she guessed the essential, but when he had told her the details, she had to put her head between her knees to stay conscious. It was Margot who realised who was responsible, it had simply not occurred to Fred that it could be Theo. But he knew how badly he must be hurting to have acted like that. Margot told him to leave, helped him pack a bag and then had gone to hold Theo who was sitting silently on the edge of his bed. Lucie had cried hysterically at the sight of her dad walking out of the house, she had tried to stop him, then got angry with Margot and Theo for making him go. They had had to explain, it was impossible to hide. Margot was so stunned that she managed to get through it all as though it was somebody else's problem, as though it was happening to one of her patients, not to her own family.

Fred had gone through that nightmare and then he had been obliged to face that meeting in the morning. His comfortable life had been wrenched away from him, all for the sake of a long pair of legs and hungry blue eyes. He felt stupid and humiliated, but then he had nowhere to go and Emma wanted him and had shown him in no uncertain terms just how much. She was insatiable. She wanted it all the time. She came on a sixpence. He felt drunk with sex, and usefully it occupied his mind, stopped him thinking about the rest. The first weekend he spent in her flat, he had woken up again to her mouth around him, half an hour later they were up and out, running fast along the lake. That afternoon they had taken out the stand-up paddles, in the evening they had climbed to a beautiful spot with a bottle of wine to drink as they watched the sun go down past the red tinged mountains opposite. They had made love where they were, there was no one around and then leapt down the mountain like goats. They ate in a little bistro where there were no children in sight and continued on to a piano bar which Fred had no idea existed. They had swayed together on the little dance floor, sauntered back to her flat and made love again. The next morning, they were up early, ready to walk to a climbing spot in time to see the early morning chamois and have time to do a few pitches before it got too hot. They got home in time to work a little in the afternoon before discussing it over a salad and sitting down to watch a film which had just enough erotica in it to push them to making love again, exactly where they were, with no risk of interruption. As they headed for bed, Fred looked back in amazement at his weekend. It had literally been his perfect weekend, he had done so much, including all his favourite things. Since he didn't seem to have much choice about where he was, he may as well enjoy it, but for the moment he needed sleep.

Since then, there must have been sixteen such weekends and Fred was really getting used to them. He was so much fitter, he had time to get his hair cut properly and buy himself clothes. He had time to himself after work, no ferrying of kids, no homework to help with, dinner to cook, sinks to unblock or political arguments over a bottle of wine with his wife. Emma was definitely not interested in politics, or theories, or his kid's troubles at school. She was a glass half full person, which meant that she simply ignored anything troublesome or negative. She concentrated on things like recipes for vinegar, a new origami model or where they were going to climb at the weekend. He wasn't sure what she read, but it seemed to give her an endless supply of sexual inventiveness and whenever there was a lull in their conversation, she found another way of occupying them. But how he missed his kids, and Margot. He could only hope that time would heal the rift with Theo. Lucie would be happy to see her daddy come what may, he was fairly sure of that, but he wanted to avoid causing any problems between brother and sister at all costs. He knew

Emma didn't really get it, how could she since she didn't have kids herself. Obviously, she couldn't imagine having a kid of fourteen, what was he thinking of sleeping with a girl of twenty-eight? But then she would walk past him naked and confident and he would stop asking himself questions. Life is always a compromise and, on some level, he believed he had the right to be happy.

"Hey babe, I'll cook tonight, I'm planning a little something special for later."

'Something special' in Emma speak probably meant something he had never tried before, having fallen in love and married quite young. He hoped it wasn't too intense, special creams or a loosely tied scarf perhaps, but nothing too mechanical or scary. And she was going to cook, that made a change, although her culinary endeavours were not always as successful as her experiments of the flesh. His body reacted to the thought.

"Sounds good, eh? It will be!" Emma turned with a swish of her skirt and a gesture reminiscent of that old tennis poster as she slipped her hand under her pants to stroke her right buttock. He was mesmerised and in a hurry for the afternoon to finish.

That evening, Emma had cooked duck breast and cheesy mashed potatoes with garlicky green beans. It was a surprising choice for her, normally they ate salad or simple low-fat pasta or rice. The unexpected richness of the meal sat well with Fred, bringing a pleasant feeling of satiety which he had hardly even realised he had been missing.

"You promised a surprise?"

"I did. In fact, I want to try something new for me this time… come with me."

Fred shook off his vague fear and followed her through to the bedroom, she was shedding clothes as she went. The sight of her naked from behind would be enough to make most men walk out on their families...

He grabbed her, turned her towards him to kiss as his hands covered every inch of smooth round bottom, sliding a gentle finger up and down.

"So what can be new for you, hussy?"

"Do you realise I've never made love naturally?"

"What do you mean naturally?

"Just you and me, with nothing between us..." She already had one long leg hooked around his waist and she gracefully entwined the other one as he took her weight and she slid down onto him. He was more than ready and not really thinking. The rubber had been becoming more and more annoying, hindering rhythm and spontaneity. The first time on the beach, Emma had been so slick and organised that he had hardly noticed the pause, but he was not so practised himself. He had not had to bother with condoms for years.

"Lie me down, I want to see your face. Look at me." It was so straight-forward that he complied, she knew how to talk during sex, how to ask for what she wanted, but this was different, slow and powerful and it felt like an act of love.

"Wow!"

"Wow indeed. Incredible. You are incredible."

"I love you Fred, do you think it might have happened already?"

"What? What might have happened?"

"You know, we might have made a baby."

"A what?"

"You know, small cute thing with sweet toes."

"Hold on, I thought you were on the pill. We never talked about babies."

"To be fair we never talked about anything, everything just happened and no, I've never been on the pill, why did you think that?"

He could hardly say it was because she seemed so free and easy about sex. This was one of those times when he realised how different in age they were.

Chapter Two

Theo was seriously pissed off, somebody else had just heard about his dad. Was there really anybody left in the school who hadn't heard? And why couldn't he just have left or even had an affair with his mum's best friend? No that would have been horrible, he really liked Jan. But to fuck Emma, whom he had been dreaming about for months. He knew she was too old for him realistically, but his dad was definitely too fucking old for her. They'd met at a family day out ironically. A team building day in a tree adventure park. The sight of the harness around Emma's ass would stay with him forever. To begin with he'd followed her, hypnotised by the sight, but then somehow, he had gone first and turned to watch her as she hurtled down the zip wire towards him. Her nipples pushed against the tiny top she wore, her blond hair swung in the wind. Her long legs were unencumbered by her equally tiny denim cut-offs and stretched out towards him. Then she had stumbled on arrival and he had caught her and steadied her and fallen in love. She had been so sweet, had kissed him thank you on his, as yet, still smooth cheek and he had definitely felt her breast brush against his arm. But that was before, it was all finished now that his fucking dad was fucking her. He felt the by-now familiar shudder of revulsion. How could his dad have done that? How could she have done that with his dad? He's so old. He's married. He's his dad. Fuck.

"Hey Theo, I could use your services…" What now?

"Like what?"

"Well, I heard about…"

"Yeh, yeh. Just leave it will you?"

"No, it's not like that, it's just that I need to get somebody back. Could you crack his website for me like you did for your dad?"

And so it began, a small business in spiteful attacks, quite lucrative and oddly satisfying. Every time it felt like another stab at his dad.

Margot was finding her patients more and more demanding. The ones who were really ill or really old or really in pain were easy to cope with, but the ones who moaned or warbled or exaggerated, tested her patience to its limits. The day she had come home and seen Fred sitting in the kitchen with his head in his hands, she had instantly known what had happened. Not the details obviously, but the substance. She and Fred had always been so open and at ease with each other. They'd been together since college — she had been eighteen and he nineteen. They had met at a dance in the student union, been friends and lovers and shared a bed ever since that very first night. In fact, he was only the second man she ever slept with and she had really thought he would be the only one forever more. She knew she had been working long hours and neglecting him a bit. But he worked long hours too. Maybe their love life had been a bit slow, but it was nothing that a summer holiday wouldn't sort out. And once she had passed her exams and become a district nurse, she was hoping to work fewer days a week. But he couldn't wait, could he? He couldn't put up with a bit of a rough patch. He had fallen into the arms (or between the legs, being a man) of the first pair held open for him.

That first afternoon she had practically felt sorry for him, he had looked so wretched, but now she was angry. What pathetic behaviour. With a girl who was nearer to Theo's age than his, well almost. And a colleague. What was he thinking? Rationally she knew he hadn't been thinking. Rationally she could have forgiven him, probably. But Theo had seen to it that forgiveness, and especially forgetting, were not quick options. As a result, she felt numb, no feeling left, just irritation with normal life. She had had to cope with a distraught Lucie as well as try to deal with Theo's pain. Her own feelings had no time or outlet, so she buried them as deep as she could.

The initial crisis was ebbing and they were starting to find life normal again, stuff needed doing for school, Margot had deadlines for her own exams, Lucie had her first traumatic period, even Rufus the dog had a swollen ear that needed attention. The relentless, heartless conveyor belt of family life. Margot's final dissertation was due in six weeks, she put her head down and became a model of efficiency. There was no time for a glass of wine in the evening, no one to distract her with suggestions of a walk or a restaurant. It was quite soothing and definitely calmed her fury. When she lifted her head from her books, having given a very well-received presentation, she looked carefully at her son and didn't like the look of what she saw. His hair was lank, he had some huge red-ringed blackheads on his nose and his forearms seemed so thin and white. Worse were the pallor, the black shadows under his eyes and the dull expression in them. She hadn't been managing his pain at all, she had been coping with her own. She felt gut wrenching guilt slice through her. She'd found time for Lucie, the tears had been demanding, but the silence and retreat had been much easier to ignore.

Lucie was sick of crying, fed up with the tang of salt in her mouth and seeing a horrible reflection in the mirror. It was time to get her dad back and Theo and her mum for that matter. She knew she had an old Barbie stuck in the back of her wardrobe somewhere. She had always hated Barbies. This one had been a birthday party present from a girl she had been obliged to invite last year. She fished it out, looking with scorn at the pointy feet, already misshapen by wearing heels. How anybody could wear high heels willingly was beyond her. Why would you teeter when you could leap and run? But the pink cliché was just what she needed. The Barbie was already dressed in a vest and short shorts. First, she cut its hair very, very short. She knew her dad preferred long hair on his women. Then she rummaged in the bottom of the messy sewing box and found some old-fashioned, big-headed pins. Considering her prey, she decided on a gradual approach. One pin at a time, nothing too obvious, this first one she bored straight into the plastic doll's right hand. It was difficult, but she relished the effort.

Rufus shook his head slowly. His ear was still itching. He collapsed with a great pflump under the table, his head lying gloomily between both paws. He was getting used to the signs which definitely meant no decent walk for him in the near future.

Fred was wondering whether to text Margot, he needed to see the kids — and her. He wondered how she was managing to walk poor loopy Rufus in the morning before work. Usually that was his job. He knew he couldn't wait too long before seeing Theo. The hurt they had inflicted on each other was still raw, but he didn't want the wound to heal over with pus underneath. And if he didn't know what was going on, on a day-to-day level with his family, they would grow away from him. They still needed him, they must. He wondered who was helping with their maths, when they had last had pancakes, if Lucie had cut her hair too short. He picked up his phone and opened up the thread to Margot.

"Who are you texting?" Emma was slicing up fennel, she was proud of her quasi-professional chopping skills.

"Nobody." But his eyes were riveted to his screen, desperately hoping for an immediate response. He wanted to go and see them all, then and there. He missed them just too much. In his haste, his text was clumsy.

"No!" he slammed his phone down on the table so hard that it bounced.

"Aah! Careful, ow!" In her fright Emma had sliced deeply into the soft skin between her thumb and forefinger on her right hand. The knife clattered to the floor as she pressed the wound with her other hand. The blood spurted upwards impressively.

Fred leapt into action. Finely tuned first aid skills and a fair amount of experience, meant that he had Emma's hand bound and them both on the way to the hospital very quickly. Emma, hustled and in pain, pushed the initial cause of the incident out of her mind.

Margot was angry too, the text had been so matter-of-fact, as though nothing had changed. As if everybody could be polite to each other, they should all just morph into a new civilised relationship, no cross words, no bad feelings, no shitty fucking betrayal. She caught herself and stopped, there was no point in getting angry with a telephone. She needed positive action, maybe her phone could help after all.

"Kids?"

Vague mumblings came from respective bedrooms.

"Cinema? Popcorn? James Bond? Leaving in ten minutes?"

"Okay, Mum." Both kids recognised the suggestion for the lifeline that it was. Normally they would go and see big new blockbusters en famille, well tough. He'd left them, no film, no popcorn and no family outing for him.

A brown-skinned, ponytailed James Bond who seemed to have a predilection for both men and women was certainly different.

"Did you like it? They've really shaken things up with this new one, haven't they?"

The three of them were wending their way back to the car, walking off their once monthly McDonalds.

"Nothing stays the same, does it?" Theo looked young and wistful.

"We had a nice time though, it was funny — what about that bit with the dolphin?"

"You're right Mum, it was a good laugh, my face hurts from smiling. I thought I'd forgotten how!"

"My little Lucie, come here." Margot put her arms around the shoulders of her two kids, holding them tight as they headed for the car.

Emma was agitated, she couldn't even make a fortune teller with her hand in this state, let alone one of her graceful swans. She hadn't realised what a calming influence, a bit of paper folding could have on her. But then she couldn't brush her teeth properly, text easily or even get the milk out of the fridge. She was feeling very sorry for herself and decidedly unsexy. But surprisingly Fred had come up trumps and actually taken some initiative in the bedroom. He had tied both of her hands gently to the bedhead and proceeded to take her mind very effectively off the pain and the ugly useless bandage. Very surprising and very promising!

The evening spent with his mum and sister had done Theo good. The next morning, he got up early and bundled Rufus out round the fields at a trot. Rufus had looked at him quizzically to start with, but he was very quickly won over by this new change in routine. Theo had decided that he didn't need his dad and he would make sure that his mum would be all right without him too. He would help, easy things like walking the dog, and he could do DIY stuff surely or cook some pasta. He would continue with his hacking business so that he never had to ask for money again. He needed to smarten up his appearance and improve his grades. Nobody ever suspected the well-scrubbed hard worker, especially one with a nurse and a teacher for parents. Once he had a routine established and a bit of money put away, then he would teach his dad another lesson and possibly That Slut he was with as well. Unless he could have her himself, that would be cool retribution. But then again, he couldn't imagine going where his dad had been before and he would definitely have to have some more experience first. Even though his plan was long term, that seemed ambitious, because he was fairly sure that That Slut had an awful lot of experience of that sort. He would have to come up with something better than that, but he had time, plenty of time. For now, he would concentrate on looking after what was left of his family.

"Come on Rufus, keep up!" Rufus bounded up, willing but out of practice. His tongue was down to his knees and his tail was whirling like a windmill, but his eyes were shining with grateful happiness.

Chapter Three

Another week had slipped by, work was hectic and every meteorological excuse possible had already been made for the students' behaviour which was just plain diabolical. As they got more and more wound up, the inappropriate comments about him and Emma slipped out more and more often. The other teachers were getting very fed up with having to fend off questions about them. There was a vague feeling that if teachers could behave in such a woefully immoral way, then why should the students themselves follow rules and regulations? They picked away at the chink in staff morale, sensing the disapproval of many of them and that they couldn't bring themselves to whole-heartedly support their colleagues. The chink became a gap and the challenge was on to make it into a chasm. And of course, there is nothing stirred-up students like more than a challenge.

The school director called Fred into his office.

"Fred, this can't go on. You are going to have to make your relationship with Emma official, make it clear that you have left your wife and that she is your new partner. It's hell on wheels in those classrooms at the moment and them thinking that Emma is your bit of stuff on the side is making it worse by the day. None of them are concentrating, they are all too busy fantasizing about what you got up to the night before and wondering if, crudely put, she is up for it with you, could she be up for it with them? I can't be doing with it any longer and I'm sorry if you are not ready to make the commitment, but it's either that or one of you leaves. I would struggle to replace either of you, mid-way through the year like this, but I would rather try and do that than continue in the present atmosphere. We will have no authority left at all by Christmas otherwise."

Fred was grateful that it was the end of the day, he couldn't bear the thought of walking into a classroom with that little speech rattling through his brain. All he wanted to do was run home to Margot, have her hold him, have Rufus put his big daft head on his lap and relish the smell and feel of home, even of wet dog. But he couldn't, he wasn't welcome any more, he no longer had a home. With sharp cutting realisation he knew that the most important thing was for the three of them, four really, to still have a home and if he lost his job, that would be at risk. How had he got himself into this mess? He had absolutely no one to talk to about it. His best friend had been distant, Bernie loved Margot like a sister, he was Lucie's godfather. Fred knew that his loyalties had been sorely stretched. His parents didn't even know yet and he couldn't talk through the details with them. They would never turn their backs on him, but he wasn't going to burden them with too much knowledge. The head was right, he wasn't ready for the commitment, he probably never would be, but what could he do? His choices were stark, he needed his job, if he split up with Emma now, she wouldn't take it lying down, the atmosphere at work would be terrible and he would probably get sacked anyway. If he wanted to keep his job and keep a home for his family, he would have to publicly acknowledge his relationship with Emma as being serious and committed. At least one person would be happy, there was no doubt in his mind that Emma had decided that he was "the one" at least for a while. She had even been making jokes about having a baby the other night, crazy.

So the next morning to Emma's delight, Fred padlocked their bikes together outside the school, picked up her bag as well as his own to save her bandaged hand and put his arm around her shoulder. He was well aware of the nudges and snickers coming from every corner, but that was it, done. Five minutes into the first class of the day, came the question, put bluntly as only teenagers can.

"Is Miss your new squeeze then, sir?"

Fred was prepared and, to be honest, pleased to able to step back into an honourable place rather than putting up with all the innuendo, "Emma is my girlfriend yes, I am living at her place until we can find a new one together."

The head had been right, the basic truth when it was given straight to the students, greatly improved the conditions in the classroom. They could no longer snigger and embarrass — their collective strength had been deflated. Thankfully their relationship had become the affair of adults again. At the end of the lesson Fred headed for the staff room, Bernie was obviously waiting for him.

"We need to have a beer after work, your goose is well and truly cooked."

"I had no choice Bern, but a beer would be great. Just what I need if fact."

"I'm sure you do my friend!"

Fred wasn't sure what Bernie would have to say later, but already the atmosphere in the staff room was lighter. Somehow, they could cope with a dalliance which apparently had some serious intent whereas the previous uncertain, saucy scandal had been unbearable.

Word spreads so quickly and gossip even more so. By the middle of the morning at least five people had shuffled over to Theo to see if he had heard. Which of course he had. His pocket had been vibrating all morning. He just wanted to cry, to go home and see his mum, at the very least put his head in his hands, but he couldn't. He wasn't going to let them see him beaten and anyway it was a temporary blip. He was going to sort everything out.

Margot had also heard. A seemingly well-intentioned comment from a patient who happened to be one of Fred's student's parents, had put her very clearly in the picture. Her gut response was anger, how dare he do something like that without even warning her? Anger was good, it gave her some energy and strength to cope. Quite frankly she was sick of Fred and his behaviour. She had never envisaged life without him, but for the moment it seemed to be a fairly pleasant option. It was time to start making some plans which didn't include him. They needed a holiday for starters and Fred would have to take Rufus. They would go and stay with her uncle in Spain; some family beach time, even in March, was just what they needed. She could almost taste the salt. She picked up her phone to send a message to her uncle who, although elderly, was up-to-date with emails and even 'WhatsApp'. That done, she started thinking about Christmas. It was still a few weeks away, but she needed something that would distract them all from the change in their circumstances. An advert, which seemed to be reading her thoughts, appeared on the right of her screen. House swapping, brilliant, very cheap and original. It was also brilliantly absorbing, now that her dissertation was finished, it would give her something to dream about. People seemed so generous and trusting on the site, it was positively heart-warming…

Lucie was starting to feel a bit better, but she was still just as determined to carry on with her plan. She had seen a blurry photo of her dad and Emma on Snapchat. They were arm-in-arm which she hated, but the cheering thing was the big white bandage she had spotted on Emma's right hand. She dug out the Barbie from the back of the cupboard and grabbed a pin from the little pile she had collected the other day. She was tempted to stick it right into one of those cones that pretended to be breasts, but she was a little bit scared. After all, it seemed to be working and she didn't want to go to prison for murder. What about a little way into the stomach? She knew about the agony of period cramps now and a really bad period couldn't be blamed on her. As a bonus her dad wouldn't be going anywhere near that bit of her for a while at least. She had better take the other pin out, that way no one would guess what she was doing. Mission accomplished, she sat down at her desk and applied herself to her homework. She didn't want anybody's pity or being treated kindly because her dad had left. She was going to make sure it was business as usual on that front so that her dad would be proud of her when he came back.

Theo was feeling quite cheerful, he had been for a run with Rufus every day for the last ten, his spots had nearly disappeared, his hair was less greasy and he had made a useful amount of money. But as he approached school his cheerfulness vanished, there was a group of unpleasant looking guys in the corner smoking and generally giving off a menacing air. He had seen one of them earlier in the week hanging around outside his house and he had a feeling he had been watching him or at least keeping tabs on him. He had a feeling of déjà vu as the one he had seen stepped aside from the group and greeted him with a snarl. He had huge muddy boots on, his jeans were rolled up to a strange height and tightly slung around his body was a white Adidas flight bag.

"Yo Thomlin…"

How did he know his name? What did he want? Theo felt like running, he could possibly get past them and into the sanctuary of school, but they would definitely be there when he came out and that would be worse.

"Um, hello."

"Yes hello, Theo." A much leaner guy stepped out from behind the one who had spoken first. He sounded less threatening and was dressed more normally, jeans, the latest Timberlands and a green hoodie with a beanie pulled down low over his face.

"Sorry I have to go, I'll be late for the bell, they'll give me detention this time, sorry." Feeling quite relieved by what had come out of his mouth, he lifted his hand in a half wave and picked up his pace, heading as quickly as he could without it showing for the school gates.

"No worries, we'll catch you later." Of that he had no doubt…

When Fred got home, having drunk two beers more than his usual limit with Bernie, he was quite relieved if he was honest, to find Emma curled up with a cup of tea under a duvet on the armchair next to the radiator. He recognised the posture and the pale, wane look. Also, he had been married for long enough not to let her know that he had guessed what was the matter.

"Hi, are you okay? What's up?" After hearing Bernie's frank opinion on his future, he had not been feeling like living up to Emma's usual erotic demands. Coping with common or garden period pains felt like a much easier option.

"I feel awful, could you get me some ibuprofen and a glass of water?"

"Oh, poor you. Is it what I think it is?"

"Yeh, I don't usually get it like this though. I'm not sure if I'll be able to work tomorrow."

"Really? I've never known you miss a day on the hill before. Do you want me to ring Vincent so he can replace you?"

Fred and Emma were both teachers at a school which combined technical teaching with mountaineering and skiing skills. It was an ideal job in many ways, the challenges of teaching combined with two days a week hill walking, climbing or skiing depending on the season. It wasn't perfect, the hours could be long, the students could be de difficult especially in the classrooms and the pay wasn't great, but it was a pretty good compromise. It wasn't easy for a young woman to have got the number of qualifications necessary to be a fully functioning member of the team, but Emma had done it. And she definitely hadn't done it by wimping out once a month. Fred wondered if it meant anything, but he could do sympathy and tea, especially if it meant that one unprotected slip up or in, or whatever, hadn't had any consequences.

"Could you blame my hand do you think, say I slipped and made it worse or something?"

"Of course, just sit tight, I'll sort it. Don't worry, everyone knows you love that route and the weather forecast is great for tomorrow, there is no way it looks like an excuse."

"Thanks, I just don't think I could do it."

Chapter Four

Margot had started her practice. She'd been lucky in that an old friend, with whom she had worked years previously, had managed to get pregnant after years of unsuccessful IVF. When her precious baby finally arrived, she had decided that there was no way she was going to miss the first important years. Originally, she had offered Margot a locum position, but now she was pretty sure that she wanted to sell the practice or at least share it. Professionally, Margot was over the moon. It was perfect, near home, it wasn't full-time and there was the possibility of earning a bit more by doing extra work at the old-people's home if she wanted. Best of all, they had agreed between them that they would keep the workload down so that they could easily take longish periods off.

She had also organised a house swap with a nurse's family in Edinburgh for Christmas. They could leave Rufus in exchange for looking after her two cats. EasyJet was still quite reasonably priced and her mother could come too and they could even pop over the border to Carlisle to visit her sister. Margot was born in Cumbria, but her parents had moved to France when she was eleven. Although her dad had died five years ago, her mum was settled and happy to be near Margot and her family. The kids had never been to Scotland and she was sure they would love the Christmassy atmosphere. They had agreed to leave a decorated Christmas tree in each home. It was so much quicker just deciding things on her own. No 'ifs' and 'buts', just do it.

At the weekend she had to admit she was lonely and missed having company, but she was so mad at Fred that it wasn't him she missed. When his name cropped up, she felt the hair at the back of her neck prickle with annoyance, a slight film of sweat break out round her hairline, followed by a squeeze in the area around her left breast. Okay so maybe it was her heart, but it was an angry heart. Luckily her studying had left her feeling confident. When she had gone to university, straight from school, it had been a question of learning to pass exams, but this time with the experience and wisdom of age, she had studied in order to understand. What a difference, she felt as though her brain had literally expanded. She was capable and knowledgeable and inspired by her new job.

Perhaps it was time to do a bit more physically though. She had weighed herself at the new surgery and she didn't think she could put all the blame on her jeans. And her hair was lank and in need of something. It was naturally a light chestnut colour, but the shine had gone, making it just a dull brown. She hated going to the hairdressers, but it had to be done. Maybe she should try a more up-market one than usual, just to see if they could work a miracle. She could call it a reward for finishing her studies. She was also going to start running again, straight away, and start some stretching first thing every morning. One way or another she had let things slip, but she was going to take herself in hand. She could still look at herself naked in a mirror without too much shame, but only if the light was right. If she was honest with herself, she had to admit that her self-esteem was pretty battered. She had seen a picture of that girl, but she wasn't going to compare herself, it wasn't even just age, but she hadn't ever been that stick thin, straight up-and-down, even aged eleven. Why should she compare herself anyway? She could remember clearly how much Fred had loved her body in the past and it was a fairly recent past at that. And he had always been generous with compliments. He was kind, intelligent and he had seen the babies they had conceived, slide out of her. That hadn't put him off her, it had felt like the opposite. Forming a family had been a natural thing to do for them, it was who they were. She still couldn't believe he had thrown that away.

Her mind had drifted back to Fred as usual. And as usual she had to pinch her inner arm hard to make herself realise that the reality was that Fred had gone. Her Fred, the other half of Fred and Margot, had gone. She had seen her own disbelief mirrored in the faces of her parents and their friends. It was as if they had been the last couple to give hope to the happy-ever-after dream. Perhaps she needed a night out with girlfriends, but did she? She didn't want to hear anybody else's opinion about Fred's behaviour or that somebody had always thought he was this, that or the other. Because he wasn't, he was a lovely man and she couldn't believe he didn't love her any more. She had seen the longing for home in Fred's eyes when he had offered to help the last time they had Facetimed, but frankly he was going to have lie in the strange bed he had made for himself for the foreseeable future. What they had been together had felt so solid. Now she was going to have to get on with her life, fill it up with different things, but she didn't want bitchiness or bitterness to be part of it. She had just stretched out her hand to pick up the phone and ring for an appointment at the hairdressers, when it rang. It was her friend, Jan, they had met outside Theo's infant school on his first day and had instantly forged the kind of friendship which was lasting and instinctive.

"How are you, Margot?"

"I was just about to make an appointment for the old life-changing hair-cut."

"Brilliant, are you going to try that new salon?"

"No, in the end I'm going to stay with the tried and trusted, but change style and get some colour, the whole hog."

"You'll get in more quickly anyway. Listen I have a plan."

"I don't know, I've just decided I don't want to go out with the girls…"

"No, it wasn't that, I was pretty sure you wouldn't fancy that. I was going to suggest a day in a spa, hammam, massage etc. I've never done it, neither have you, have you? It would be cool, a complete change."

"Oh Jan, you know what, that would be perfect. Just the two of us?"

"Just the two of us, we might even have time to finish a conversation!"

"Bliss! When?"

"You say, then you can go to the hairdressers after that."

"Saturday then?"

"Yes, yes, yes! Lucie can come and play with Marion and we'll all have pizza together in the evening at our place. Theo and Max will be okay with that, I'm sure. Pierre wanted to do some gardening, so he won't mind."

"It'll be nice to see Pierre, it feels like ages, in fact I haven't seen him PF."

"PF?"

"Post Fred…"

"Oh god, PF!"

Jan cackled and Margot joined in, suddenly full of

optimism. Saturday would be great.

Emma was feeling her breasts, she had been hoping that her last period having been exceptionally heavy may have been a sign that her body was ready and receptive. Although she had supposedly started taking the pill on the first day of that period, for some reason, a fortnight later, there were only six empty blisters in her packet. She just kept forgetting to take them. Now she was hoping she felt a little bit pregnant, but her breasts seemed as small and as taut as ever, in fact it was just turning her on. She had to get to Fred quickly when she felt like this otherwise, she might do something rash. She shot off a quick explicit selfie. No need for words.

Fred was busy though and when his phone pinged, he was in a meeting with the parents of an errant sixteen-year-old. He had forgotten to turn the sound off and he cursed himself as the image of familiar uninhibited breasts flashed across his fortunately small and hidden screen. It didn't turn him on at all, it just flung him straight back to Theo's photo-shopping on the timetable. Talk about unprofessional, she knew he was at work. He thought of Margot, she would laugh at him for getting into such a ridiculous situation. Well, no, she wouldn't, not in the circumstances. She would never do anything so demeaning or find herself in such a tawdry situation. Oh god, what was he doing? He had to tune back into the depressing, depressed mother of a socially-inept, fat, teenage boy. He couldn't help feeling that if she had just fed him a bit better then they wouldn't be sitting here having this conversation, but hey, when it came to parenting teenage boys, who was he to say?

Theo was thriving, he had sorted out a vendetta for the threatening guy who had kept turning up outside school. It had been risky, he had dumped some evidence on someone's Facebook page and then contacted the moderators who had in turn contacted the police. But now he had protection of sorts, nobody was going to make life difficult for him as long as he stayed in the good books of Eli J-J. He had built up stamina from running and some muscles from doing lifting exercises he had found online. He had discovered the wisdom of smiling, if he smiled, the world smiled back at him. He built up a repertoire of jokes gleaned from US comedy sites. He had spent some of his money on a hip haircut and some cool T-shirts. He was working at school, just enough to float around the top of the class. He hadn't kissed a girl yet, but he could feel their interest growing. He would take it easy, build up the demand, make them wait. He had a plan and he was quickly learning how much a bit of focus and drive could bring you.

He still had his black moments though. Sometimes he was scared. Sometimes he hated the lack of morals and decency in his customers and therefore ultimately in himself. And sometimes he just missed his dad and the normal old days so much that he could feel himself on the very edge of crying.

Margot and Jan's spa day was unexpectedly good. They had started giggling almost immediately and as the day continued, they just got worse. The final steam bath and rows of leathery old men with little, strategically placed towels was the final straw. They clutched their sides and their towels, laughing until it hurt. It wasn't a very polite place to laugh so much, the expressions on the other user's faces told them that. It only made them worse. Calming down enough to head for the showers, they vowed to make it a regular outing.

"Oh my god, I feel like I haven't laughed like that in years." Jan's eyes were still wet from tears.

"Me neither, I feel like I've had a real work-out."

"It must be good for us!"

They smiled at each other, looking forward to the uncomplicated family evening ahead of them. Margot realised that her life could carry on without Fred and that she and her family could still enjoy themselves.

Chapter Five

Suddenly they had all made it through to March and they were packing the car for the trip to Spain to see Margot's uncle. Lucie decided a little action was called for and quickly stuck a pin right through the shoulder of her battered, butch-looking Barbie and hid it swiftly in the disturbing nest of unidentified soft stuff under her bed.

Theo had his affairs in order, his great uncle had internet anyway so he could keep an eye on anything he wanted while he was away. He was happy not to have to see those shifty, scheming faces around him for a while. Two weeks break, by the sea, surrounded by beautiful Spanish girls in bikinis, what was not to love? But then his dad turned up to pick up Rufus. He looked the same superficially, but all the details were different. His hair, his shoes, his sunglasses perched stupidly on his forehead — a necklace for god's sake. Theo still couldn't face him, he turned back to his room closing the door firmly.

"Two weeks on the beach Margot, sounds just your thing!"

"Should be, did I tell you that I've booked kite-surfing courses for us all?"

"Wow, I've always wanted to try that, why didn't we do that before?"

"You don't like sand, Lucie was too small, we didn't have enough money, there was…"

"OK, I get it, I just hope you all have a brilliant time."

Margot smiled sheepishly, after all he was only being friendly.

"Anyway, Uncle J is paying — or something, I think the kite-surf guy owes him for some work he did on his school or some such."

"That's nice of him."

"He's a lovely old man, I think we'll try and go a bit more regularly, he needs some company and I can help him with bits and bobs while I'm there."

"It'll be good for the kids Spanish I suppose."

"They'll probably find kids who speak English too. I'll see if we can take Rufus another time."

"I'm happy to have him of course, it's just not having a garden which complicates things, and the upstairs neighbours."

"You could always stay here."

"Really?" Fred looked amazed.

Margot suddenly realised why, she'd forgotten about Emma for a moment, it had felt quite natural chatting to Fred in their kitchen.

"Just you, idiot! Not both of you!" She slapped his arm gently and, incongruously, they laughed. Rufus pricked up his ears and lolloped towards them and to his delight, they did it again!

Theo couldn't believe how much he loved feeling the wind pick up the kite and pull him. It was the fourth day of the course and the conditions were perfect. It felt even better than he imagined flying would feel. Lucie had a bad morning, the board had bashed her on the back and then she had fallen just one too many times. She had had enough of kite-surfing for now.

Theo picked up his board and made his way back to the

base. He looked around for his mum, but she was nowhere to be seen. Lucie was sitting on the sand looking out to sea.

"She's there!"

"Wow! Look at her go!"

The instructor sauntered over to the two of them. "She's pretty unusual your mum! You too Theo, you did really well."

"Not me." Lucie grimaced.

"You, Lucie, did exactly like most people, you just need to keep going. But your brother and your mum seem to be really quick learners."

"It's fantastic, I want to be a kite-surf instructor, I want your job!"

Uncle J was ambling down to meet them in his battered old shorts, leathery bare feet and misshapen straw hat.

"Heh, heh — good investment, Jaime. I told you it was a great plan. Now Lucie, did you know that Jaime's sister has a hacienda with some very handsome Palomino horses? And I know she is always keen for an extra hand around the stables and some help exercising them. And it is only ten minutes on your bike."

"Uncle J!" Lucie rewarded him with a grin that made his eyes suspiciously wet and a hug that made him blush.

"I'll tell Olivia you'll be over this afternoon around two, shall I?" Jaime was grinning at the unusual sight of the normally stoic Julian squirming with pleasure under the onslaught of his bonny great niece.

Just then Margot whooshed onto the sand with a beach-stop worthy of an expert. After four days?

"Pick your jaw up Jaime!" Julian chuckled, amused to see his cocky young friend so taken aback.

"Whey! How come I've never tried this before Uncle J?

It's out of this world. Wow!"

She dropped onto the soft sand and lay spread-eagled in her wetsuit, ecstatic, exhilarated, but also exhausted. Jaime was back in charge,

"Come on, no lying around, we've got to get the gear rinsed and put away. There is an ice-cream with your name on it when you've finished."

By the end of the second week of staying in Uncle J's cute little beach-side villa, Theo and Margot were hooked. They were buzzing with the wind, the salty sea, the adrenaline of their boards starting to soar over the waves. Lucie was also in heaven. Her ultimate aim was to be a vet, preferably a vet who did her rounds on horse-back. It seemed an obvious idea to her, it would be ecological and good publicity. Two weeks amongst those noble Palominos were just what she dreamed of. She felt part of the stables and her Catalan was getting there. Halfway through the second week though, she had suddenly become really worried about Rufus. She needed to know if her dad was looking after him properly. It was so strange not to know what her dad was doing. She asked her mum to text him, she still wasn't talking to him. The news about Rufus was reassuring, there had been no problem about leaving him for too long on his own because Emma was off work. She had slipped while doing some bouldering and broken her collar-bone.

Margot saw Lucie's face go white under her tan when she told her this news, and sympathised. Why should that woman get Rufus as well?

"Can we bring Rufus with us next time Mum?" Lucie asked.

"I don't see why not. I think Uncle J would love him."

"So would Jaime!" giggled Lucie, she was convinced that

Jaime had a massive crush on her mum. "When will we be back Mum? Olivia and Manté want to know."

Mantequilla was Lucie's favourite, he was shorter than most of the other horses and a real softy with a massively thick white fringe. The beige skin on his nose was the softest thing Lucie had ever touched. When she whispered in his ear, his whiskers trembled and he blinked with eloquent sympathy. He knew everything. She couldn't bear to be parted from him for too long.

"We'll come for Ascension, there's a five day break then. Uncle J says it'll be fine."

"Whey for Uncle J!"

Just then Theo jogged in, he'd stopped walking anywhere, it was too slow and pedestrian. He ran in sandy places and skateboarded everywhere else. His chin was squaring up, his hair was blonder and his previously greasy lank skin was tanned deep brown. He had not only grown, but broadened in the last two weeks of intensive physical activity.

"Mum, Luce, Uncle J — guess what? Jaime says I can enter a competition this summer if I can train enough."

"Fantastic, we really need to buy you some kit to take back with us. Even if the lake is not exactly like the sea, it would be better than nothing."

"Actually, he says he's going to come round with some stuff tonight — for both of us!"

"What? We can't afford it for both of us."

"We have to, he says you are going in the veterans' category. And the more people from his school who enter the more points he gets and you might win because there are very few old biddies entering."

"Theo!" Uncle J intervened, "You mean senior women,

don't you?"

"Me in a kite-surfing competition? Are you all mad?"

"Come on my girl, you know you're a natural. Give it a go!"

"Go Mum!" Lucie could feel more time for her and Manté on the horizon. And it would be one in the eye for Dad and his mountain running Slutface.

And just like that, their lives changed course, again.

Uncle J had enjoyed life before, but he had been lonely at times and achy. His house had been starting to look as dusty and battered as his old hat. Margot had sorted him out. Now he had a massage every two days and his house cleaned and washing done once a week. He had a regular appointment with a chiropodist, whose cousin came and cut his hair and gave him a wet shave at home once a fortnight. The masseur was a mad keen kite-surfer and fifty euros a week to ease the aches and pains of a leathery, fit, grateful old man kept him in food, beer and a rich supply of usefully clean jokes. Julian couldn't believe how Margot had organised such change in his life. She had instinctively known what he needed. They WhatsApped frequently which was fun, ridiculous photos zapping backwards and forwards. Knowing they would be back soon had made all the difference.

Four and a half weeks later, they were back, with Rufus this time. They slipped instantly and naturally back into the new lives they'd made for themselves.

Chapter Six

Fred had loved having Rufus around again, Emma not so much. She couldn't get used to the smell, the mess or the time constraints. Fred restrained himself from telling her that a baby would be all of that to the power of ten. He didn't really want to bring up the subject of babies. She had wanted to go away for an impromptu stay in a refuge, but he had to say no because of Rufus of course. He made it up to her with a couple of romantic restaurants, but still.

Emma's collar bone was knitting, she could run and cycle again, but climbing was off for a while. At first, she had been shocked by Fred's obvious lack of enthusiasm for a little baby of their own, but she liked a challenge in her men. So she agreed to go on the pill, in fact after a couple of horrific periods, her doctor had advised it. But pills didn't always work, did they? She hadn't liked having that great hairy, slobbery setter around either. It was a relief when Fred had taken him off for a few hours. Once they had got rid of him, she would up her game, her shoulder should be better by then. She had a good plan for the weekend, maybe she would be a bit absent minded tomorrow about remembering that little yellow pill. On the other hand, it felt great to be getting back into shape and having a baby now would put that in jeopardy. Still, it didn't do to plan life too carefully, it really wasn't her way. As she cycled home from work, her phone rang. It was raining and cold so she didn't want to stop on the way up the hill, if it was important, they would leave a message. In the end it was a couple of hours before she remembered to pick it up. It was her friend Linda, the message crackled with excitement and enthusiasm.

"*Hey Emma! We're on, we're doing it! We can't wait another year or we'll never do it. I saw Mika at the weekend and she is up for it. Chloe answered when I phoned her before and it is perfect timing for her. In fact, she said it might be the last time she would be available. Too many competitions next year or something. You know Chloe. Anyway, ring me back asap. You've got to say yes!*"

Emma looked at her phone with surprise. She had not been expecting that, but she had no doubts. Life had a way of making decisions for you if you let it. She punched the air with excitement. And clicked on Linda's number.

Fred had been over to the house a few times while his family had been away. He'd mowed the lawn, cut back some shrubs, fixed a tap and a hinge and pressure-hosed the alley. It felt good to be back, solid and useful. And by chance, he was there with Rufus when they drove in and piled out of the car, scattering sand. They were smiling, brown, happy, filled with pleasure at the sight of Rufus bounding towards them. He was engulfed by a longing to have them back, to belong with them again, to be greeted in the same way as Rufus.

But Fred had to tear himself away. Lucie and Theo had shuttered down as soon as they caught sight of him. The holiday happiness had suddenly been eclipsed. It hadn't escaped him how beautiful Margot had looked either. Beautiful and relaxed, in spite of being the only driver after a long journey. She had been friendly and grateful for the things she instantly noticed he had done, but he knew he had to leave quickly. He drove back to his practical, boringly furnished flat, without even his faithful dog snuffling in the back seat, feeling dead inside.

That evening Emma dragged him off to the piano bar they had gone to during their first weekend together. Fred was thankful for the distraction. They danced and she looked stunning. It was romantic and sexy. She told him she had a surprise planned for the next day and, after a leisurely brunch in bed, they were on their way towards Geneva. They were going to a spa, it was a hammam and a sauna with access to the lake. It was popular among the young and beautiful cosmopolitan population who lived on the shores of Lake Leman. In the spring there was a strictly no clothes policy. It was hot, the birch saplings used for scraping impurities from the skin were surprisingly erotic and the cool fresh water of the lake felt exquisite. It was a very new and different experience for Fred. He could see the admiring glances Emma was getting from men and women and his ego liked it.

The weekend had been as satisfactory as Emma could hope for, they had made love more times than she could remember and on Sunday they had walked up to a mountain chalet, eaten delicious potato cakes and salad and ran back down. That evening, as they opened a bottle of wine and sat on the terrace, Emma told him about her plans for the summer.

Ever since their student days, Emma and three of her best friends had promised each other that they would cycle the length of South America before their thirtieth birthdays. She wasn't the only one of them to be feeling maternal and they had suddenly decided that it was now or never. Emma had no intention of giving up on the dream of babies either. They would be gone for five months, mid-June to November, not long really. She had already checked the conditions for a sabbatical at work. It was on. She was about to buy the tickets.

Fred's emotions were all over the place, the weekend had put him into sensual over-drive, it had been amazing and then suddenly Emma dropped her bombshell. He couldn't believe that she had planned something so important without out even discussing it with him. Equally though, he was relieved by Emma's news, because surely this meant the issue of babies had been shelved. A few months break might give him time to win his kids back, but he couldn't help feeling pretty disposable. Emma hadn't seemed to consider him at all in her decision making. He couldn't decide how he felt about that. His life was a mess, but maybe there was a little bit of light at the end of the tunnel.

Lucie wasn't sure what to do next. Her mum seemed happy and fit, but she wanted her dad. If only he could see her mum like she was in Spain, then he would drop that stupid slut straight away. She had hated not speaking to him when they got back from holiday. All she had wanted to do was to run into his arms and tell him all about Manté. She couldn't though, Theo was so angry with him still. And she couldn't just forgive him for what he had done to their family either. She knew she couldn't expect her mum to just take him back as though nothing had happened even if it was an option. She wasn't as naive as everyone seemed to think. But she had seen her mum wiping her eyes as she carried the bags into the house, she was sure she still loved him. What should she do next? She didn't want That Slut to be getting too much sympathy from her dad. She knew from past experience how good he was at that. She would have to wait and see. Think a little. She was pretty certain of her power. Somehow, she would get her dad back where he should be.

Theo, meanwhile, had other things on his mind. He had met a beautiful and very cool Dutch girl. She had a fringe like Manté and her mother ran the beach bar. Facebook was keeping them in touch for now. It did have positive uses after all.

Chapter Seven

The summer term was drawing to an inglorious end. Everybody was too hot to work and just hoping to get out into the sun, or leafy shade, or cooling lake water. Basically, longing to be anywhere other than in the sweaty, stuffy building in which they had spent the last year. Lucie was doing well at school and dreaming of spending the summer with Manté. She and Theo were going as soon as school finished, by train. It would be a proper grown-up adventure. Uncle J was coming to pick them up at the station which was about forty-five minutes from his villa. There were two changes and the whole journey would take about nine hours. They would be with Uncle J for nearly three weeks before their mum joined them. Theo was equally keen to get back to Lotta and excited by the idea of travelling on their own by train. He had been kite-surfing as much as possible and training in every other way he could think of. He had kept his grades up at school and his nose clean. The only dark moments were when Eli J-J demanded his services. He tried to do just the job asked, not to use much imagination and not think about the consequences of his action. He still missed his dad, but he was also still angry and disgusted with him.

Fred was wondering what the summer would bring. He was going to be alone, Emma was leaving half way through June, his family and dog were going to be in Spain. He would have to find something to keep himself occupied. As usual on a Thursday he was having a beer with Bernie before heading home.

"I have had this amazing offer for the summer."

"Tell me…"

"Well, I've got this mate I was in the army with who is looking for someone to be in charge of a group of young prisoners who are due out on parole. They are going to build a sustainable mountain hut between Val Thorens and Orelle. It sounds right up my street, but I can't go, Sophie would never forgive me. Imagine if I abandoned her for the summer with the kids."

Fred tuned back in at the idea of being abandoned for the summer.

"Oh sorry, Fred that is what is happening to you isn't it?" Bernie laughed. He still hadn't really accepted his friend's new life.

"So what appeals to you about the project then, Bernie?"

"All of it, helping those poor kids, spending the summer up high, getting fit…"

"How high is it?"

"Two thousand three hundred I think."

"It'll be harsh up there, even in the summer."

"Imagine the sunsets."

"And those lads will be townies, won't they? How will they cope?"

"They've coped in prison, they are going to be able to cope I'm sure. Some of them are skilled workers and some of them have learnt new trades while they've been inside."

"How long is it supposed to take?"

"Five weeks, I think. It's quite low budget, the whole idea is to be fairly Spartan and to learn to work as a team."

"And you fancy that?"

"Well yes, five weeks creating something new, giving them a chance. Do you know how many of them go straight back inside when they are released? At least this way they will have no access to drink or drugs or contact with their old cronies. And they get paid so they will have a little bit of a buffer when they do go home. Normally they find themselves let out with no bed, no money and little hope of a job. This has got to help."

"I suppose it does sound like quite a good idea. But are you allowed to work with kids over the holidays as well as in term time?"

"They aren't kids, they are all in their twenties, so it's okay."

"So if you are not doing that I suppose you are off to Sophie's parents' house as usual?"

"To be fair, we love it there. So do the kids. You can't beat a month of surfing for washing away the woes of school. And Sophie's mum loves cooking which just makes it all so easy. I go and do some bulk shopping every three days, and she does the rest. Last summer I plumbed in an extra dishwasher in the garage and bought a second fridge and it all just works!"

"What's not to love?"

Fred wandered home feeling dejected and envious. Bernie, Sophie and their four kids would be spending the summer as it should be spent. How could he even imagine giving that up to go and work with a bunch of criminals?

Emma was re-packing yet again when he got home. It was tricky, obviously her baggage had to be minimalist and as lightweight as possible. Every time she thought she had it sussed, she panicked that she had forgotten something. Fred did a double take when she stood up and turned around to greet him. She had had her lovely curly hair scalped. It was about a centimetre long; he was pretty sure he could see her skin through it. Where there had been glossy colours, there was a kind of nothing colour.

"Wow!" He gulped, trying to stay non-committal. "That is some hair-cut!"

"I just love it! It feels great, try!" She grabbed his hand and made him stroke her head. He tried not to shudder, he had always hated the feel of velvet, it made the hairs on his arms stand on end.

"It'll be practical I suppose."

"Yeah really, much less sweaty under a helmet. I was going to have just a bit cut, but the hairdresser persuaded me to try this. He said it was now or never, that it's a young woman's cut. So I went for it and I can't believe how much I love it." She crossed over to the mirror to examine her reflection, posing like a model.

Fred shook his head and decided he really needed another drink. He went to get them both a glass of wine. He held it out to her, but she grimaced.

"I should be in training Fred and I haven't finished packing yet."

"Just one…"

"Okay, santé."

"You know you can always buy things over there if there is something you need."

"I'm not sure about that."

"Of course you can, you'll be going through some towns."

"I suppose, I'm sorry, this must be annoying. What are you going to do while I'm away?"

"I'll find something, don't worry about me." He knew her well enough to know that she wouldn't.

The next morning Fred woke up to Emma re-doing her bag yet again and suddenly realised what he was going to do with his summer. If it was still possible, he was going to help a gang of ex-cons build a hut up a mountain. Perfect, it was worthy, high altitude, healthy and above all woman-free!

It took one phone call. The project had been on the cusp of being abandoned through lack of suitable leadership and Fred had the right kind of profile to allow it to continue. He had no experience with prisoners, but the kids at his school had a solid reputation as mischief makers and that would do. There were three other staff members who were prison guards who would rotate, but he was the one with experience both in the mountains and in dealing with lads wielding tools. He would walk them up, oversee the building work and walk them back down at the end. Food, water and building materials would be helicoptered in every couple of days.

It was exhilarating, it made his heart beat faster. He had no space in his mind to question Emma's departure. He had decided that he was going to live day by day for a while and let the rest of his life settle around that.

Chapter Eight

Emma's friends were a mixed bunch. Emma herself was super-fit, but Chloe was a semi-pro cyclist who lived for her sport. Linda was a sports teacher also, but she relied on natural ability, being much too much of a party animal to train seriously. Then there was Mikela who had gained a little weight recently as her job as a cook in a ski resort had started to take precedence over her love of the sport. She was no longer a ski bum who cooked, she had become a chef who skied on her days off. Fortunately, they knew each other's foibles inside out, they had flat shared for five long years at university. They were all equally motivated, they had even found a few sponsors. Mikela's restaurant had coughed up, the idea of their chef doing a sporting challenge appealed to them. Chloe's normal sponsors had come through. Then suddenly Linda met the father of an ex-pupil in a club and, over strawberry mojitos, he had made her an offer.

"We all wear Go Pros and you'll give us ten thousand euros?"

"That's it, we should be able to get a food advert out of it."

The girls were over the moon, they could put their savings back in the bank for when they got back. Just before packing hers away Emma had an idea.

"Fred, come here. We need to try these Go Pro. I'll wear it the first time and then you. It'll give us something to keep us going while I'm away!"

"What? No way! God knows where it'll end up."

"Oh, don't be so old, it's not exactly the first time…"

"What? I hope you're joking! Who are you, Emma Bartolini?"

The end of term festivities were paid lip service to. Fred had tried again to make peace with Theo and Lucie by attending a school fête, but it had been a waste of time. Whenever he approached, they scuttled off like deaf, blind hermit crabs. He had had a reasonable conversation with Margot, but she too had looked uncomfortable. It was true that none of them wanted to be reminded that they were subjects of so much gossip. It had been a stupid idea to show up at a school event. When he got home that night, he emailed both of the kids to let them know what his plans for the summer were. He decided that from then on, he would be up-front with them, treat them as individuals. Honesty and openness had to be the best approach. At least emails could be pondered, re-written, re-read and replied to when the spirit was moved to do so. He'd asked Margot to tell the kids he would be emailing them. It wasn't a medium either of them used much. He hoped that keeping the lines of communication open would be enough in the long run.

Eventually Emma left in a flurry of lateness, due to last minute panics. At least it made Fred realise what a big deal it was for her, because she had hardly been making passionate declarations about how much she would miss him. She had been too busy WhatsApping her friends for the last three days as they consulted over arrangements, plans and details. The door closed finally and he sat down heavily in front of the telly, opened a beer which had mysteriously found its way into his hand, switched to some football and watched it mindlessly. He tried to analyse his reactions, but frankly he had no idea how he felt. One day at a time, that was all he could do. He had a week before his mission started. He would run in the morning with Rufus and do odd jobs at home after that. He could swim in the lake on the way home. Margot would be at work and the kids had left yesterday. Satisfied and strangely peaceful, he opened another beer and shoved a frozen pizza in the oven. At least it was organic according to the box.

Margot was looking forward to being in Spain. Like Theo, she had been training, not to his extent, but still. She loved the control she was starting to get with the second-hand kite surf she had bought and couldn't wait to try it out on the sea. Her job was going really well, her patients seemed satisfied and pleased to see her. She had invested in a very efficient accounting app for her phone which seemed to take care of all that side of things almost on its own. Also, it would be quite nice to have the kids out of the house for a couple of weeks. She could eat more simply, do a bit of long over-due spring-cleaning. She could even go out if she felt like it.

The day before Fred was due to leave, he turned up to mow the lawn. He had been every day to take Rufus out even though it was a forty-minute drive, but that morning it had been raining and he hadn't been able to cut the grass. It cleared up in the afternoon so he decided it was worth the risk of driving back so that he could leave things as he wanted. It had got quite late in the end and he was only half way through when Margot came home. He was hot and sweating, the morning rain had increased the humidity. Rufus was lying flat on his side just where he needed to cut next, pink tongue flopping to the ground. Intelligent dog that he was, he had never seemed to understand the concept of grass already cut and grass waiting to be cut. Margot got out of her car with relief, it had been a difficult day. Her elderly patients had been grumpy because the break in the hot weather had been so brief. They were suffering, tired and unwilling to look on the bright side.

She laughed as Rufus hauled himself to his feet yet again to lumber out of the way of the approaching mower. It felt like coming home. Even though she had been happy to have a break from the kids for a little while, it was a bit lonely coming back to an almost empty house. Fred was looking good she noticed, fit and tanned. And hot.

"Hey, thanks for doing that, Fred, you didn't have to."

"Hey yourself. You know that I absolutely did have to! How was your day?"

"Y'know — hot, sticky, everybody a bit tetchy."

"Yeh, it's certainly hot."

"Would you like a beer?"

"Well, are you having one?"

"I'd love one and I feel odd having one on my own."

"Deal then! I'll just finish this corner and put the machine away."

"Okay, I'll just get out of these work clothes."

A quarter of an hour later they were sitting in their usual spot drinking a beautifully cold glass of beer. And chatting quite normally. There was still a mighty pachyderm swinging its trunk wildly, but they discussed companionably their summer plans, the kids, the garden, Rufus, their parents, friends and whether or not they wanted another beer.

"Why don't you stay and eat, it's getting late. Have a shower, eat, sleep in Theo's bed and then you can take Rufus for a last run in the morning. You've already driven miles today."

"God, that sounds so cool. Although I think I would prefer Lucie's."

"Up to you!"

"Thanks, Margot."

Even though Margot knew she still felt angry and betrayed if she dug deep, they had a normal easy-going evening.

"You know what, Margot, I have decided that the only way I can cope with this mess I've made is to go and do this job and just take each day as it comes. I mean who could have foreseen this?" He indicated their empty plates, the candle flickering in the breeze, Rufus lying firmly on both of their feet.

"Do what you have to, Fred. I'm not sure with two teenage kids that it is possible to avoid facing the future, but for the summer, let's give ourselves, all of us, a break."

"Exactly, stop thinking, stop worrying, we'll just be and do!"

"And kite-surf!" Margot didn't want the mood to darken or deepen, she could see the wisdom of Fred's thinking.

"Yeh, I have to see you kite-surf. I can't believe it."

"Cheeky, I'll have you know that I'm going to enter a competition." She was now anyway.

"No!"

"Yes! Over forties, veteran women. Jaime gets more points for the club for every competitor. "

"Wow, that's fantastic. Well done you."

Margot blushed, happy to be praised and poured them another glass.

"You'll have to come down to Spain, meet Lucie's Manté

and see how Theo is in his element." But that was one comment too far, they smiled at each other a little forlornly and stood up to clear the table.

"So, are you going for Lucie's bed?"

"As long as that is okay with you?"

"It's fine, it's time I hit the sack and I need to text the kids."

"Okay, I'll just take Rufus down the lane and I'll see you in the morning. I'll be up early, I haven't really packed yet." He grabbed the lead and was out of the door almost before she could answer.

"Right, sleep well." And that really did feel strange, but she appreciated him getting out of the way while she took herself off to their bed.

Fred lay awake for hours looking at the glow stars he had stuck on the ceiling years ago. He was going to have to work really hard about not thinking about the future after this evening.

Chapter Nine

Emma had a terrible flight. She hadn't been able to sleep at all and unusually for her she'd had to go to the loo at least five times. It had been embarrassing, but she had no choice. The next day they were taking it easy, putting their bikes together and buying a few provisions. The serious stuff would start the morning after. When she was rudely awakened by the extremely annoying tones of 'Highway to Hell' which Linda had decided would be an amusing alarm for their trip, she felt dreadful. Her head was leaden and her limbs stiff.

"It's just a bit of jet lag, you'll be fine once you start pedalling." Chloe did not believe in being too soft.

"Hopefully, I didn't feel like this when I went to New Zealand."

"It's age, m'dear." Mikela was philosophical and quite grateful for somebody else being below par.

The next morning Emma woke up feeling hungover even though none of them had touched a drop of alcohol the night before. When she moved her head, she thought she was going to throw up. She lay still and the feeling gradually abated. Chloe was already doing press-ups. Mikela groaned.

"I thought women were physiologically incapable of doing those. Like we didn't evolve to need that action. How many has she done now?"

Linda had been counting in awe, "Thirty, should we all just go home now?"

"Don't worry, it's not a race, it's a journey. We'll be fine once we're on our way." Mikela was not only philosophical, but optimistic.

"A journey, eh? Capital J I suppose?" Linda cackled.

"Oh, shut up, just find me breakfast."

Breakfasted, to some degree at least, and packed, they put on their helmets.

"Okay, let's stand in a circle and we can each switch on our neighbours Go Pro and make a pact. It'll be good telly. I'll get the guy at the desk to film us at the same time." Linda quite fancied some reality TV kudos.

"Good grief, let's get a move on then."

And so, looking quite ridiculous in pristine cycling gear, camera-enhanced helmets and shiny bikes, they made their pact and kissed each other before swinging their legs over as they started, what they hoped would be the adventure of a lifetime.

Like many adventures, the beginning was rather mundane. They had to cycle through the traffic and suburbs to get clear of the city. They were hooted and whistled at continuously. Chloe was incensed.

"Have they never seen women on bikes before?"

"Look around Chlo, can you see any other female arses sticking upwards in stretchy Lycra?" Emma just found it amusing and usefully distracting as she tried to find her cycling legs. "It'll be better once we are out of the city."

The first day was a short one, they knew it would take a while to find their rhythm and that Mikela might need some nurse-maiding. In fact, both Emma and Mikela were exhausted at the end of the day and very grateful that they had booked the night's accommodation in advance. Neither complained, but it was obvious to their friends that they were struggling.

"How are you feeling, Em?"

"I'm fine really, pretty shattered though. This jet lag is a pain."

"You should be better by the morning."

Luckily the hotel had a nice easy restaurant, they ate and slipped early into their beds, even Linda.

Fred had arrived at the prison. He was definitely intimidated. He supposed it was normal for it to look just like a prison in a film. The clang of the door behind him was enough to make him swear to stay on the straight and narrow for life. Not that he needed much incentive for that, on the other hand he was an adulterer now and in some cultures that was classed as a crime. Once he was through the formalities, he started feeling a little less apprehensive. He was introduced to the chain-gang, as they were affectionately (he supposed) known, in a normal classroom. And they looked like a pretty normal bunch of guys. There was the usual variety, some spotty, some lank, some brawny, some nerdy, some cool and the inevitable peacock. He had their names in ten minutes and was starting to feel more confident. The director of the prison turned up to give a pep talk. They all had their liberty at stake, it was as simple as that. There could be no rule-bending, no trouble of any sort whatsoever. And no second chances. It was crystal clear and Fred felt a little more confident. He was enough of a realist to know that it wouldn't be a walk in the park, but somehow the inherently intransigent nature of the deal seemed to make it likely to work.

"Have any of you been in the mountains before?"

There was a general shuffling of feet and shaking of heads. Fred felt a slight surge of optimism, hopefully they couldn't help but be awed by their surroundings. The naughtiest, slyest boys at the school where he worked shut up and listened when faced with a vertical drop or a sudden blanket of impenetrable fog.

"What about building? Any trades among you?"

This time the response was more positive, they all had some experience and most of them a qualification.

"It's a simple construction really, but it has to be strong and well insulated to stand up to the weather conditions up there."

"Is there water?" Fred was pleased to get an interested question.

"The site has been chosen next to a stream, so we'll be able to build a filter system which will make it drinkable."

"How long will it take to walk there?"

"It'll be about four hours the first day and six the second, we'll bivouac on the way up."

"Two days of walking up?" "You're joking!" Fred laughed at the horrified exclamations.

"Don't worry, it's beautiful and we'll take it easy."

"Mate, some people pay good money to do this!" One of the friendlier looking guards joined in.

"Well, are you coming with us then, Big C?"

"Actually, I am, looking forward to it to be honest. A couple of days in the fresh air, away from this place. Even if it is with you lot of moaning minnies."

Fred was relieved, Big C looked like it would take more than these kids to worry him and he looked fit, even if he was carrying a few extra kilos.

"Ha! We'll see who moans first!"

The afternoon was spent organising kit. Fred had refused

point blank to take anybody into the mountains who was not properly equipped. They needed proper footwear, fleeces, water-proofs, sleeping bags, water bottles and rucksacks. It cheered the prisoners up to get a load of new gear for nothing and a real sense of anticipation rumbled through them.

Fred was still relieved to step out of the prison door at six o'clock. He was spending the night in a hotel nearby. They were leaving at nine the next morning. The supplies would be dropped off, tents included, at four p.m. the following day. It was doable but there wasn't much leeway. Tonight, however, he was going to have a beer or two, a nice meal, some wine and a hot bath. And then he would text Margot. He wanted to know how the kids were getting on. Instagram shots of Emma and her friends flashed up frequently telling him all he needed to know about her.

In St Pere, life had quickly settled into a routine which suited them all. Everyone did their bit. The four of them took turns in cooking, with the condition that nobody ever complained about the food. This meant that Theo could heat up frozen pizza if he wanted, Uncle J could spend hours following complicated, authentic local recipes, Lucie could vary her pasta dishes a little and Margot provided them with the real taste of home every fourth day.

Rufus's routine was casual, but there was always somebody walking somewhere, so he just tagged along. He had made friends with a whip thin dog at the kite-surf school. It was more than friendship, it was his first real puppy love. He wasn't so welcome at the riding school where his general loopiness could have unintentional consequences, but Lucie made it up to him with extensive grooming sessions every evening. She had even given his tummy a number two shave to try and keep him cool. She sang to him as she shaved and brushed and hoped that he wasn't missing her dad too much.

Every so often someone else would join them to eat, but they would always bring something and Julian made sure they knew the rule. Jaime dropped in quite regularly, he would come on Theo's day with take away pizzas or foil wrapped kebabs on the back of his moped. Margot was happy, she still had some domestic responsibilities, but they had managed before she got there and there was no real need to change anything. So, she took a step back and alternated between running or a yoga group on the beach first thing, followed by buying food and organising the renovation of Julian's villa which would take up the rest of the morning. The villa was quaint but overgrown and slightly crumbling round the edges. Julian had touched nothing since the day his Donna had left twenty years ago. He had been a little bit heart-broken, but he hadn't enjoyed the nagging compromises of coupledom either and had whole-heartedly embraced a lifestyle free of domestic trivia. The villa had started as charmingly cluttered, but over the years had become sadly scruffy. Margot was gently rearranging and repairing. The young kite-surfers, with whom she spent her afternoons once the wind got up, were a wealth of skilled labour. In return for a meal or some advice about a dodgy rash or sore elbows, she could get most jobs done. Uncle J was looking groomed and smiley, he was relishing the company and the bustle. He had even started doing a little stand-up paddle on the calm morning sea. He would wander down to the kite-surf school with Rufus, and Jaime would carry a board down to the water's edge for him. Half an hour later, he would step off, leave his board on the shore, whistle for Rufus and wander back for a coffee and siesta before lunch.

Lucie was still totally smitten with Manté and her riding was improving daily. Being on the beach so often made her at ease with the changes in her body. She was skinny and blond which helped, as did the complimentary comments from the kite-surfers. They were gallant and kind, it was like having a bunch of protective big brothers looking out for her. Not that Theo did much of that. Theo was too busy to bother about his little sister, he was in love with life, Lotta and most of all kite-surfing. He was strong now for his size and his balance was excellent, having skied since he could walk. As a bonus, he had exceptional wind sense which came completely naturally to him.

"Did you know that my grandad was a sailor?" Margot was sitting in one of the comfortable cane armchairs on Uncle J's terrace with a glass of rosé in her hand. She had strung up some solar powered fairy lights and found pretty hippy chic cushions to mix with cheaper supermarket ones. The terrace was perfect in the fading heat of the evening. They each had a favourite spot, Theo preferred the hammock, Julian had his own armchair moulded to fit him by years of use and Lucie lounged on an old sofa, stroking Rufus's ears.

"Not just your grandad, your dad and I did a lot of sailing ourselves when we were young."

"I didn't know that."

"Actually, he could have been very good indeed, but you know what happened, he fell in love and moved inland!"

"Not just inland, but to the mountains."

"Well, you know how the wind goes round in circles on those mountain lakes. It's hardly worth getting wet."

"True and money was always a bit tight when I was little. Sailing is an expensive sport, I can't imagine Dad having enough for a boat."

"Exactly, but it doesn't matter, he was happy in the mountains and being a family man, anyway look at the two of you carrying on the family tradition."

"That's pretty cool, Uncle J. So it's not so weird that Mum and I are good? It's in our blood." Theo lay back looking at the stars feeling part of the place and at peace in a way he couldn't have imagined a few months ago.

As she got ready for bed, Margot looked at herself in the mirror and almost did a double take. She looked so different, she had muscle tone, she was tanned, her hair was streaked and unruly and her face had relaxed. 'What would you say, Fred?' What are you doing?'

Chapter Ten

Emma was pushing her pedals round with a faint air of desperation.

"Tired, Ems?"

"Bushwhacked, why am I not getting used to this? It's not as though I'm not fit."

"It must be that tummy bug that's making you so weak. You threw up again this morning, didn't you?" Chloe was harsh, but right.

"Wait a minute!" Linda pulled level with their bikes. They were on a long straight stretch which should lead them to a small village where hopefully they would find a bed and a shower. It was two days since they had either and the fun of bivouacking and cycling in the humid heat was wearing thin.

"You were sick again this morning?"

"Emma! Are you being sick every morning?"

"And you're exhausted…"

"Emma!" The chorus came from all three of them as the slow penny plummeted its way into its deep slot. Emma wobbled, nearly fell off and then came to a sudden stop.

"What? What are you all on about?"

"Pregnant Emma, expecting, in an interesting condition…"

"Up the spout?"

"Bun in the oven?"

"Okay, okay, stop, no, not now."

"We'd better see if there is a pharmacy in the village."

"Oh my god." Emma felt weaker than ever and they still had to get to this ever more distant village.

"Let's just pedal, get there and then see." Linda was always practical. Mikela gave her a quick sympathetic rub on her shoulder, Chloe was already twenty metres ahead.

The village turned out to be only another two kilometres further on. With great relief they quickly found its small hotel, where they took a room for all four of them. The room came with the bliss of its own shower. Linda let the others go first and wandered off to look for a pharmacy, she was lucky as the village was just big enough to have one. By means of her rudimentary Spanish and some explicit gestures and more money than she had expected, she got what she had come for. She quickly returned to the room holding an innocent-looking brown paper bag. Silently, she handed it over to Emma.

Emma was wrapped in a towel, sitting on her bed. She pulled the test out of the bag.

"What answer do you want, Emma?" Mikela was worried by her subdued friend.

"I have no idea, this wasn't the plan, not now, not at the beginning of our trip."

"Well just do it, then we'll know, maybe it will be negative and then you don't have to ask yourself anything." Chloe was irritated, she didn't want to have to change their plans. This was meant to be for the four of them, something they had talked about for years, they were all old enough to look after their own bodily functions. They weren't innocent teenagers any more.

"Can you do it now or do you have to wait until the morning?" Mikela was feeling more and more anxious as Chloe's annoyance was becoming increasingly obvious.

"It says any time, but maybe I should wait until the morning." Emma wasn't sure she could cope with knowing the result yet.

"No way, do it now." Linda wanted to know, then she could get on with handling the situation.

"Yes, now, then we'll know." Chloe was not in the mood to be patient.

"Listen, I will do it in a minute. Why don't you and Linda go and have a drink downstairs, will you stay with me Mikela?" Emma knew they were right really, not knowing was not good. Twenty minutes later she was sitting on her bed again staring at the blue line on the little window. Mikela was sitting next to her holding her hand.

"Oh god, it's true, I really didn't think it could be."

"What will Fred say?"

"Oh my god, Fred."

"Had you talked about children?"

"He has children, two teenagers and he definitely doesn't want any more, but he knows I do. But not now, not here."

"He'll come round, if he loves you. Nobody can resist a baby."

Emma agreed with both comments, but she couldn't help feeling that it was pretty easy to resist a huge bloated pregnant whale, especially if you hadn't wanted one in the first place.

"Can you go and tell the others? I think I'm going to go to bed, I'm so tired and I need time to process."

"You should eat…"

"I can't, I'll be all right, I just need to think and sleep."

"We'll talk in the morning."

Emma had already turned her head towards the wall and closed her eyes.

Fully occupied, Fred was trying to suss out who was responsible enough and competent enough to help manage the project. If he couldn't trust them to do the job, he may as well put the hut up himself. They had a chores rota sorted, but no one was showing an interest in the plans he had spread out in front of him. Hopefully once they got going with the construction it would become obvious who knew what they were doing. For the moment, they were all just moaning. The previous night had been cold and damp and their legs and backs were aching from the walk up the mountain. There had been some excitement when the helicopter arrived to drop off the materials for the hut, but even that had been physically tough. There was only one place where they could receive them and that was the future site for the hut. This meant that as soon as one load landed it had to be carried off site to the side and onto a more steeply sloping terrain. It felt and was dangerous. At least it was done. They had the bare bones of a high mountain hut and a sheet of instructions which owed more to Ikea than Lego.

"We'll try and get a good night's sleep, lads. The forecast is good for tomorrow, so we should be able to get a good start."

"We should get those showers set up, that pond is freezing."

"You're right," Fred was glad to hear something constructive. "Let's start by getting the camp properly set up in the morning and then we can start building."

Fred was worried about the general mood and unsure how to lighten it. He didn't want any violence to surface. His main hope was that once they started grafting, the physical tiredness and satisfaction of seeing work in progress would settle them down. He was going to use climbing as a carrot. He would take them one at a time to do some easy pitches. He had to reserve some energy for that as well. As he lay down that night he thought about Margot and how she had always heard the kids crying during the night, way before him. He hoped he would hear if anything happened, but he had to sleep otherwise he would be no use to anyone. Luckily the stress had worn him out and he didn't stir until five a.m. when a ray of sunshine fell over his face. He opened one eye and saw two figures sliding back into their sleeping bags. 'Of course, prayers before sunrise,' he hadn't thought of that. 'Lucky them,' he thought, 'having someone to turn to for advice and support.' He felt very alone and very aware.

"Right Fred, what next?" Big C had got everybody up, organised breakfast, its clearing up, and was rightly pointing out that some kind of routine working day needed to be established. Fred was mindful of the main goal of the operation so he called a meeting.

"Right lads, we need to decide who does what and how we're going to do this."

The guys looked very surprised, they weren't used to having their say in matters. Some even looked slightly scared, one or two looked distinctly relieved.

"So you won't be pointing a finger at somebody every evening to tell them you're fired, will you?"

"God, it's not even just fired, we'd be back inside sooner than you can set fire to one of Big C's farts..."

"Any stupidity, violence or all the other things that the boss told you before and you will be on your way back, but not for just making a hash of things."

"And anyone coming anywhere near my behind with a lighter will also be going down in more ways than one." Big

C could take a joke, but he needed his authority to be unquestioned.

"I know how to read the plans, if I have a couple of people to help me, we can get the bottom framework laid out and we can see where we go from there and work out where the foundations need to go."

"I can lay foundations."

"You know we don't have a mixer?"

"That's okay, Rapha and Matis will be good at shovelling and mixing... plenty of practise."

"Hey!"

And so it continued, until they had sorted who would be doing what and at the suggestion of Andy, who looked like he was probably the one the most concerned by the question, they had worked out a cooking rota for the next few days at least. It was a successful, encouraging discussion and they set about their allotted tasks with willing. The next couple of hours went well and it was already time to eat. As they sat around on the various stones they had collected, eating a couscous salad which was really not too bad, Fred looked over the valley. There were big black clouds building up, he had the feeling that progress was going to be hampered imminently and long hours lying in the small tents were probably coming up. He hoped they'd all learnt some patience in prison, or at least some good card games.

Chapter Eleven

Storms had put paid to any kite-surfing in St Pere, kites and lightning were definitely incompatible. Theo was getting more and more nervous, he knew he had got to move on from just being friends with Lotta, but he just didn't know what his next move should be. There were times when he really missed his dad, not that he could imagine how the conversation would have gone, but quite often his dad had seemed to casually bring up the very subject that had been troubling him. He wasn't all bad, he supposed. But that made him think, should he really let a woman, well a girl, under his skin, would he lose control of his life like his dad had? Was it really worth it? It might take the edge off his kite-surfing, he might become all soppy with no competitivity. He tried to focus on how happy his mum and dad had seemed to be as a couple before The Slut, but had it just been an illusion? Look how quickly it had fallen apart.

He was lying in his favourite hammock, half-heartedly scrolling through some updates on his phone. The thunder clouds were dark and threatening, but it was still really warm and there had been no rain as of yet. Maybe he wasn't ready to take the plunge with Lotta, he wasn't quite sure what would be expected if he did kiss her. He couldn't quite imagine what he would do with his tongue if he kissed her. Porn was graphic and easily accessible, but you couldn't film inside a mouth and any close-ups of kissing reminded him of the cows in the fields next to his house when they had been drinking — very, very slobbery. And what would happen after a kiss, even supposing that worked out okay? How far should he push her, would it be obvious how much she wanted him to do? God, condoms, that seemed impossible. Disgusting, slimy, wouldn't it just make him shrivel up? A trial run for that would be possible he supposed. Just don't think about those cows' tongues.

Later in the afternoon the thunder was rumbling round, but it was still dry. Theo whistled for Rufus and wandered off to find Lotta. As usual when he saw her, all his previous worries vanished. She was a normal person, she reacted and talked and laughed at his jokes. She had been emptying the last bins at the bar, the beach having cleared with such an obvious threat of storm. They followed Rufus down to the sea, he didn't care if there were black clouds and he galloped into the water chasing a sea gull with loud happy barks. The sea gull joined in the game with mock dive bombing and noisy shrieks. Theo grabbed Lotta as Rufus shot past her, nearly knocking her over, she was finally in his arms and he brushed her hair out of her eyes with the palm of his hand. The look she gave him was all he needed to bend and kiss her as the waves broke over their feet. He kissed her just a little, but then the seventh wave broke and splashed them up to the waist.

At the same time the first spear of lightning cracked open the sky on the horizon. Rufus was not a brave dog and he did not like storms. He ran for the bar, his tail, which normally wind-milled as he ran, tucked between his legs. Theo and Lotta followed, running up the sand as the first mug sized raindrops started to fall. There weren't many at first, you could almost avoid them, but every one which hit left a dinner plate sized wet patch. By the time they got up to the beach bar, the raindrops were falling fast and thick and they were soaked.

Theo pulled Lotta under the cover of the roof and back into his arms. Her wet vest top clung to her and he could feel the tantalising hardness of her nipples and the softness of her breasts pushing against him. He kissed her again and as she put her hands round his neck, he groaned her name. The storm was strengthening fast and Theo suddenly felt something warm and hard nudging his groin.

"Rufus, stop!"

Lotta collapsed with laughter as she realised what had happened, "Come here Ruf, it's all right. He still loves you too!" Then she blushed as she realised what she had said, which took the pressure off Theo who leant over the dog and kissed her again.

"Come on, we have to get somewhere dry."

"We can't cross the beach in this, we'll get hit."

"Can we get inside?"

"Sure, the key is just here." Lotta reached up and took the key from its fairly obvious hiding place. "Come in."

It was small and functional inside in a sandy cool way. Most of the business was done outside, but there was one table with a couple of old cane chairs and a small sofa covered in a tie-die throw. Lotta got a bowl of water for Rufus and a biscuit. He was okay inside, as long as no one asked him to go back out into that thunder, he was prepared to lie down and have a snooze.

"He's a cool dog, even if he is bit stupid."

"Hey, don't call my dog stupid!"

"Or what?"

She was playing him and he knew it and he loved it. And they would have to take their t-shirts off, they were soaking. He pulled her towards him and gently lifted the bottom of hers.

She didn't resist as he pulled it up over her head, instead she copied him. They stood looking at each other and then Theo couldn't resist it any longer, he gazed at her breasts and held out a hand, she pulled his hand towards her and to his amazement he knew what to do.

They didn't make love on the grungy old couch in Lotta's Mum's bar, but it didn't matter. Theo knew that they would sooner or later and that it would happen when and where they both wanted it to. He had forgotten, in the porn-soaked world of being a teenager, that Lotta would have opinions and feelings as well. They would work it out together and it would be fantastic while waiting and even better when it finally happened. They were a bit late back to their respective homes, but even that and their wetness went pleasantly unmentioned. Apart from Lucie, who had the cheek to wink at him as she made a fuss over Rufus.

"Come here you poor wet animal, where have you been? Come and have some food."

Theo went up to shower and change and sighed with pleasure. Life had been so bad before and now it was just so good.

The next morning was pleasantly cloudy, after days of hot sun it was nice to get a short respite. The air was clear and Margot was feeling full of energy. She picked up her phone and wondered how Fred was, stuck up a mountain with a group of convicts. She'd looked up on Google maps where he was. Years of living with a keen mountaineer meant she was pretty knowledgeable about the general area. Maybe she should just text to see if he was doing all right. She swiped open her messages and her thumb hovered over his face.

"Margot, hey, how are you? Are you busy? I want to take

you somewhere." It was Jaime, he looked different.

"Where? Why do you look different?"

"Jeans, shoes, haircut, shave?"

"Wow! And why? And where?"

"No reason, it feels good on the legs and feet after all this time, you know. And I want to take you to a waterfall in the mountains, so we need shoes. There are jellyfish all over the beach after the storm, we'll have to wait for the sea to clear, so no kite-surfing today. Are you up for a walk and a swim in fresh water?"

Margot suddenly realised that a change of scene was exactly what the day called for. She went to grab her jeans and walking shoes.

"Uncle J, Jaime is taking me to a waterfall, I'll be back for tea."

"A waterfall, eh?" Uncle Julian smiled nostalgically, it was a beautiful, hidden place and Jaime's intentions were clear to the old man.

"Have a nice time, it's my turn for cooking today anyway so I'll be here for Lucie."

"Maybe you could have a little word with Theo? Man-to-man? I think he may need it after yesterday." Margot smiled at her wise uncle, both of them were well aware of the turning point that getting caught in the storm had been for Theo.

"No way, I did not sign up for parenting duties, he'll be fine without any little words from me!"

"You're probably right, okay I'm off, see you later."

'It's you who needs a little word, my dear' he thought, but wisely, he said nothing.

Margot wasn't sure that she really liked being on the back of Jamie's motorbike, but he didn't go particularly fast because it couldn't and it definitely made her feel like a teenager again. They arrived in an orange orchard and left the bike next to an old shack.

"That used to belong to my great-grandad, he used to spend the summers up here to get away from my great-grandma apparently."

"It looks pretty basic."

"In those days all they needed was a bench and a glass! He said he was guarding the oranges, but I think it was just an excuse for peace and quiet." Jaime picked up the rucksack and pushed open the gate. "Through here. It's about a forty-five-minute walk."

They followed the track which dwindled as they progressed, the only noise was bird song and the rustling of leaves.

"It's strange to hear the birds, there were hardly any when I was young, people had shot and eaten most of them."

"They are blackbirds, surely they didn't eat them?"

"Even sparrows, you could even buy them in tins."

"Horrible, was life really that hard?"

"Life was very tough, and I suppose there is no real difference between a sparrow and a sardine is there?"

"I suppose not, how come you know the English for bird's names?"

"I read a lot when I was young, I was ill for a while and it kept me occupied." Jamie smiled, "Not what you expected?"

"Guilty, you shouldn't look so exactly like a surf dude!"

"You should know by now that most of us have strange backstories. Just round this corner is a place where I have seen kingfishers in the past, so let's keep quiet just in case."

Margot would recognise a subject change when she heard

one and she had always wanted to catch sight of a kingfisher, so she stopped talking and tried to do her best imitation of a Native American tracker.

"Look!" Jaime grabbed her arm with a hiss.

"Oh!" Margot glimpsed the deep blue and rich orange, she wasn't sure if it counted as seeing, but it was closer than she had even been before.

"Come on, we're nearly there, you can walk normally again now!"

"Hey I was walking normally before!"

"This is normal?" Jaime did an imitation of her imitation which had her crossing her legs with laughter. "Here we are."

Surrounded by dipping leafy trees, there was a cool circle of water with flat rocks round the edge and a small waterfall falling into it. It fell about five metres, but not with much force. It looked approachable and appealing and they were both hot after the bike ride and the walk. They stripped off their jeans and t-shirts and slipped into the cool water. It was cool, but not cold and it felt so silky compared to the salty water of the sea.

"Bliss."

"It is lovely, isn't it? Come over to the waterfall."

They swam in and out of the fall, behind it in the green light of the cave, through the shower of water and floating on their backs next to it. It was a perfect spot.

"I'll have to get out, I'm getting cold."

Jaime pulled himself out onto the rock where they had left their things and held out his hand to help her. Margot checked herself, what was she doing? But she couldn't do anything other than hold out her hand. He pulled her up and put her towel round her shoulders, but she turned away and sat down.

He sat down next to her and took a bottle and two glasses

from his bag. He fished in it again and found the corkscrew and some of the garlicky olives he knew she loved and then a tub of cut-up Spanish omelette.

"I can't come up here without a little picnic." He offered her a glass of white wine.

"Cheers, thank you for bringing me here."

"How could I resist?" His gaze was a little too intense and little too long, Margot reminded herself that she didn't really know much about him, she had already been guilty of prejudging him. She had thought he was just young and flirty, but she had already been proved wrong about several other things, so who knew? She needed to take care, but it was such a magical spot and she felt so good in the dappled sunlight on the hot stone, having felt so bad for so long, that she really didn't want to.

Jaime was wiser than his years and although he wanted Margot possibly more than he had ever wanted anyone, she also reminded him of his mother and so he knew how vulnerable she was. His parents had divorced in a very volatile way when he was only six and his mother had been left alone and beautiful in the man's world of a small Spanish seaside resort. She had toughened up over the years and she was currently living in Valencia with a very nice cultured man who respected and loved her. Before that though, he had seen countless, ill-educated macho thugs thinking that a lovely young woman bringing up a child on her own would be only too happy to service them in return for a little financial security. There was no way he would be playing with Margot's feelings, he could wait. He was a patient, confident man who knew when to hold back and when to take a risk. That was what made him such a skilled kite-surfer.

Margot didn't know if she was disappointed or relieved that Jaime hadn't made a move towards her. But as she lay back on the rock absorbing the heat, she sighed and realised that it was a sigh of relief. She didn't want to have to deal with anything else, she didn't want to complicate her friendship with Jaime, she just wanted to feel peaceful and a little appreciation helped that. Jaime heard the sigh and interpreted it correctly. He could wait.

Chapter Twelve

Emma had surprised herself by sleeping like a log. When she woke, she was happy to see a strong internet connection on her phone. She typed in "First three mo…" and Google read her mind with a plethora of information. Then she found a site for women pro cyclists. A few pages in, she was smiling again. In fact, she couldn't wait for her friends to finally wake up.

"Wake up you guys, I have news." But talking out loud stirred up the sickness and she was thumping across the floor to throw up before she could get her news out. By the time she had emptied her stomach, Linda was handing her a glass of water and the others were all there too.

"Tell us…"

"Yes, I am pregnant, but it doesn't matter."

"I think you may find that it does!"

"Yes, of course, but I mean I can continue. It says on the net that you can continue to cycle as long as you like."

"Are you sure they mean long-distance, cross-continent cycling, not just nipping to the shops?"

"No, it should be fine, it's best to cycle in the morning, but we were all finding the heat of the day a struggle, weren't we?"

"You're right, we can just adapt a bit, the same way we would if one of us was ill or injured." Mikela was relieved, she didn't want Emma to go, she didn't want to be left by herself with the other two to keep up with.

"But can we get far enough if we slow down?" Chloe was still not impressed by Emma's lack of foresight.

"Come on, we have contingency plans, we always knew that we might have to shorten the trip for any reason and get a train for the last bit." As usual Linda was the voice of reason.

"And also, I'm not going to tell Fred. What he doesn't know can't hurt him."

"You're not talking about a drunken snog you know, you're talking about his child. Wait, it is his, isn't it?" Chloe was still a little irritated.

"Of course it's his! Charming!"

"Well, you know our Em, it wouldn't be the first time you got a little carried away when you shouldn't have."

"Linda, I'm a new woman and nearly thirty, times change."

"Yeah, yeah, well at least the present situation will probably keep you away from all these gorgeous Che Guevara types while we're away."

"All the more for me!" Mikela looked dreamy.

They set off at the same time as usual and made the same speed as they had the previous day. Of course the conditions were exactly the same, it was simply that they were aware of the situation now. They cycled one hundred kilometres less than they had planned and Emma felt fine. Maybe knowing what the problem was, was enough to make her feel better. And they were away long enough for the others to have their periods so they would suffer too. She hated cycling during her period, so that was a whopping great silver-lining.

Mikela was keeping an eye on Emma which meant that she could hold back a little and she spotted her pulling at her bra.

"What's up?"

"Everything feels tight, I can't be getting bigger already, can I?"

"My sister says that's the first thing she notices, even before she has missed a period. And she has had three already."

"Wow, amazing, one of you guys will have to lend me some stuff, until we get to a decent town with a shop."

"Are you sure you want to keep going? Don't you want to just leap on a plane and go and find your Fred?" Mikela was a romantic soul.

"No way, he'd run a mile and anyway he is up a hill with all those convicts. Imagine if I turned up there. He'd hate it. The best thing is just to see what happens, play it by ear."

"That sounds reasonable, just ignore the fact that you'll be planning child-friendly holidays for next summer. And that you'll have to put your name down at the crèche as soon as you get back, in fact you should try and do it from here next time we have some internet. Places don't just grow under gooseberry bushes you know."

"Are you serious? The crèche? Fred doesn't even know yet and you want me telling the biggest source of gossip in the town?"

"Well, that does bring me back to my original point…"

"I know, look let's just not think about it, not for now anyway."

"I suppose you could always get an au pair…"

"MIKELA!"

Fred's mountain hut was progressing well. He wasn't sure how truly beneficial it was for the lads, but it couldn't be doing them any harm. They all looked pretty healthy from being outside all day, the grey prison pallor was a thing of the past. They actually looked cleaner even though they had very rudimentary washing facilities and their clothes were getting pretty filthy. There hadn't been any life-changing moments for any of them or heart-felt repentance speeches for which Fred was grateful. The project was simply going ahead in a very practical way. He had a taken a couple of them climbing, but most of them were not very interested. The roof was nearly finished and the weather, after the initial storm, looked set to be fine.

"Okay, guys. We're going to take a day off, we have two and half days in hand, I thought it would take us till Sunday to get the building waterproof, but you've worked really quickly. So tomorrow we are going to go a for a walk. We're going to get to that peak over there and down the other side where there is a lovely little lake. We can get a swim and hopefully catch a few fish as well. Sound good?"

"The swim sounds great!"

"And some fishing, what with?"

"I've got a couple of pretty basic rods, but they should do the job."

"That's so cool, I haven't held any kind of rod in my hands for four years. I'll fish you so many trout, you'll be full until Christmas."

"I doubt that, but sounds good anyway."

"Well, yeah, didn't mean you, Big C!"

The relaxed banter made Fred realise that they really had changed. They had less permanent tension, they didn't look scared or defensive. Their eyes were bright, they accepted the idea positively rather than automatically slagging off any change to routine. They were a lucky few, but it made Fred wonder if the scheme could be rolled out on a bigger scale. But the mountains were a fundamental part of the process and there weren't that many huts to build. It would be worth the effort of trying though. He wondered how Theo was, would he ever be friends with him again? He wondered if these guys had ended up inside because of their parent's stupidity. Probably. Environment and parenting had to be the biggest factors in causes of criminality. He had a sudden need to check on Theo, surely, he wouldn't do anything really stupid as a reaction to his father's disgrace, would he? He had a phone with him, but he didn't want the lads to see him using it and that included seeing its light through the tent canvas. He would try and get a quiet moment to contact Margot sometime on their outing tomorrow, there should be some big rocks around the lake to hide behind.

Lucie was missing her dad more and more. Sometimes she felt like she was the only one who missed him. Her mum and Theo were so busy kite-surfing and hanging around with Lotta and Jaime. Even Rufus seemed not to mind that his best-loved master wasn't around any more. His life was so great here at the beach that he gave the impression of being as happy and as well-adjusted as a dog could be. She reminded him of her dad as she brushed his coat, but he just groaned with pleasure. She had whispered everything into Manté's mane as well and he seemed to understand, but it just added to her heartache that her dad had never seen him. She had to get him here, to Spain. He would see how gorgeous her mum looked, see Jaime hanging around her with puppy-dog eyes and do something. But it had to be just him, she had to find a way to get him to come on his own. She had deliberately left the Barbie at home, it would have looked really weird if she had brought it with her and also she was a bit worried as to how well it seemed to have worked. She didn't want to have too much temptation in her way. Maybe she would have to have an accident herself, obviously she could fall off Manté, but he would feel responsible and that wouldn't be fair. Maybe she could pretend to have some kind of mental thing going on, brought on by the stress of the split. That way they would have to react in her interests and her interests would definitely not involve a visit from The Slut. She would have to do some research, check what would be the easiest kind of problem to imitate. It would have to be serious enough for them to all take notice, but preferably something that didn't hurt too much.

Margot was a little worried by Jamie's intentions, so she tried to spend a bit less time with him. It didn't work though, firstly he had been Uncle J's friend for a long time and was always round the house. Secondly, Theo wanted to spend as much time with him as he could. Even Rufus seemed to sniff him out wherever they went. She just had to keep her signals of non-intent clear and try not to forget that she was the mother of teenage children, not a teenager herself. There were all those awful names, MILF, cougar and who knows which others existed these days. She caught sight of Brigitte Macron on the cover of a celeb magazine in the supermarket and cringed. But there was only, how many years difference between her and Jaime? Actually, she didn't know his age. And what about Fred? Ridiculous to even consider it, so why was she? She wasn't, it was just the heat making her mind meander or evening-time wine making her daydreams awry. It was fine, nothing to worry about, nothing to see, just move right along… What she really needed was to speak to Jan.

"Margot, hi, how are you? You look fantastic, so brown, so blond! Wow!"

"Hi Jan, good to see you. I'm great, just wondering how

you are?"

"We are all hunky dory, the kids are so happy not to be at school that they are being as good as gold. Pierre is loving having more time in the evenings with no nagging about school work and stuff. And no ferrying them backwards and forwards. First world problems I know but why do we impose them on ourselves?"

"And on our kids."

"So who is it?"

"Who is who? Who is what?"

"Don't bluster with me, I know you too well. You are ringing me up to tell me you've met someone and you don't know if you should go for it or not. Am I right?"

"How the…?"

"Language! So I AM right?"

"I can't believe you, can you really know that?"

"You are sparkling my little love, totally gorgeous and that comes from more than surf and sand."

"I haven't really met someone, well I have sort of…"

"Tell me all, no rocky details left unturned as they say."

"Are you sure they say that?"

"Stop fluffing, I have wine, I have time and now I want to know all!"

It did her so much good to laugh and talk through things with Jan. As usual Jan didn't tell her what she thought she should do. They weren't teenagers after all, but talking it through had cleared her mind and she realised that she must be very careful of potentially hurting Jaime and be very upfront with him. She would have to tell him clearly that she wasn't interested. It would be good to know his age though.

"Theo, do you know which category Jaime competes in?"

"No idea, why?"

"Just wondered, no reason." Very subtle Margot. Carry on like that...

"Well, here he is, ask him yourself. Which category do you compete in Jaime? How old are you anyway?"

"Good evening to you too Theo! Why the interrogation?"

"It's Mum, she asked."

"Did she? Good evening, Margot."

Margot blushed, good grief when had she last blushed?

"Well, I compete in the Senior Mens, I'm thirty-five."

"Thirty-five? You don't look that old." Great now Lucie was joining in the conversation.

"Well thank you señorita, so kind."

"Mum is forty-one."

"I know, that is why she can compete in the veteran category. Not just compete, but win!"

"Yeah, go mum!" He had deflected the issue beautifully and she was grateful but no closer to her aim of being clear and honest. Clear and honest with whom she wondered. She needed taking in hand; flattery and hot sun was having a strange effect on her.

"Margot, how are you?"

"Hi, Fred, I thought you were out of reach?"

"I am officially, I'm hiding behind a rock and whispering, but I needed to know if you are all okay."

"We're all fine, loving it here in fact."

"Even Theo?"

"Especially Theo, I think he is in love and not just with kite-surfing."

"Gosh! Who with? Has he told you anything?"

"You're joking! He got caught in a storm with Lotta in her

Mum's beach bar and he's been grinning from ear to ear ever since."

"Have you had 'the chat'?"

"Haven't you?"

"Yes, but ages ago, before it made any sense."

"I know, I asked Uncle J to help but he just laughed at me! Don't worry he's a sensible lad and little Lotta has her head screwed on I think."

"Okay, unfortunate wording in the circumstances, but we'll go with it. How is Lucie?"

"I suspect Lucie is really missing her dad, she's happy with her horses but she wants to share it with you."

"Oh Margot, I'm so sorry. What a mess."

"It'll work itself out Fred, try not to worry about it all, you have to keep your eye on the ball with the job you're doing. Have you heard from Emma?"

"Not directly, but they post updates on Instagram for their sponsors, so I know where they are."

Margot felt strangely pleased by this, "How is the hut looking?"

"Actually, I think it's going to be amazing, it's quite avant-garde and the lads are doing a great job. In fact, we've taken a day off today and that's how I could phone you. You'll have to stay in it one day."

"We all will, it would be fun."

"Great, that is something to look forward to. How is your training going? Ready for the big competition? I can't believe it, my wife in a kite-surfing comp!"

"Actually, it's going really well thanks. I'm amazing myself! You should see me go! And Theo of course. He's really serious about it as a sport, he wants to be an instructor."

"It's so good to hear your voice Margot, it had just been too long without news of you all. Is Rufus behaving? How is Julian?"

"Both doing great." Margot was becoming troubled by the intimacy of the phone call, it felt like they were just holidaying apart, not like they had split for good. What was he thinking?

"Maybe I could pop down, when I finish here. I'd love to see you all in action and if Lucie is missing me…"

"We'll talk again when you get back down to full oxygen levels, Emma might not be too keen on you joining us down here."

"Oh, I'm sure… hang on I have to go, something is up. Speak soon." And with that the line went dead.

Margot sat looking at her phone, what exactly had just happened there? It felt like old times. Could they just go back to where they had been? Could she forgive him and take him back? Was it just because Emma was away? How serious was he about her? If only Theo hadn't found out, they might have been able to coast around a blip. On reflection she probably didn't need to worry about Theo being careful with Lotta, he had seen what rash behaviour could do. Still, she'd better buy some condoms and leave them in easy access in the bathroom. They had some at home, had for a while, but she hadn't thought about it here. Well, she presumed they did, she hadn't checked, maybe Fred had been using them. And there it was, the hurt and anger resurfaced like a moor hen out of the water. She was still hurting, but she missed him too, she missed her best friend and co-parent. Things hadn't been bad between them, just a little rusty. It wasn't as though they'd argued or traded insults. They always been caring with each other and had their fair share of fun too. Like the man said, what a mess.

Chapter Thirteen

Emma had definitely decided to keep her pregnancy a secret, they always said that you never knew what might happen in the first three months and she really wanted to continue her trip. After all it was her body, her baby. She would much rather surprise Fred with the news face-to-face, where she was fairly sure she could distract him from any negative reactions. Even on Facetime you had to count on words, not her usual tactics. Also, she didn't want anyone at work to know and Fred might tell Bernie if he had no one else to talk to. In fact, if she had her way, and she wasn't being so sick, she would just bury her head in some nearby sand and forget about it all until she got home. She had thought she really wanted a baby but faced with the reality and all the presumptions people seem to make about having one, she wasn't so sure. She enjoyed being with Fred for example, but he wasn't always easy, what with his hang-ups and his worrying about his kids and even his stupid dog. Honestly his kids were old enough to manage without him by now. She had hardly seen her dad since she was half of Lucie's age and it hadn't done her any harm in her opinion. They got on fine whenever they did bother to get together, and there was no hassle if either of them were busy doing other things for a while. So she really couldn't understand Fred's permanent angst about his two. If he just backed off a bit, they'd be just fine without him. And another thing, could she really imagine not having sex with anyone else for the next five years or so?

However inventive she got, that would have to get routine. And she had a pretty clear idea about how Fred would react if he found out she had been with somebody else. It was another one of his little things. It was quite sweet really. All in all, the best thing to do was absolutely nothing, hopefully the sickness would clear up soon and she could just take each day as it came.

"What are you thinking about, Emma? Do you think it'll be a girl or a boy, which would you like? I mean I know it doesn't really matter, but quite often people get a real feeling for which one it is. That way you can start mentally preparing for everything, choosing names and things, painting the room. It must be so…"

"MIKELA, shut up, will you? Let's just pretend that it's not happening and let's just have this adventure we've talked about for so long without sounding like a bunch of old women!"

"But…"

"NO, no more talking about i…"

"Not even…"

"No, not even anything, nothing, zilch, end of…"

"Okay, calm down, it can't be good for the baby to get all het up."

"Good grief, I said no more!"

"Right, okay, take it easy. Do you want a cup of tea?"

"I'd love a beer actually."

"But you can't have…"

"MIKELA, I can have what I want!"

"Okay, I'll get us a beer, sit there in the shade, I'll be right back."

Emma sat down with a groan. If Mikela was a typical example of how people were going to treat her when they knew she was pregnant, she didn't think she could stand it. She was still her after all, she hadn't undergone some mysterious saintly personality transplant. If she didn't rise to the bait, maybe they would get the message and ignore the whole thing as much she intended to. She had to try and stay calm and keep the conversation on other things.

"Hey Mikela, get me one too, will you?" Linda had just walked into the hotel bar looking fresh faced and beautiful. The two old guys sitting in the corner turned their heads in unison, their false teeth at risk of falling in their drinks. She dropped gracefully onto the bench next to Emma.

"That shower was heaven, I feel normal again, like a real girl! All I need now is that beer and everything will be just hunky dory."

Mikela struggled over with the three sweating glasses of ice-cold lager knocking against each other.

"Hey, don't spill any, I need that! Why did you get three? Do you think Chloe will have finished in the shower already?"

"It's for me dumbo and I bet Chloe will have finished because you probably used all the hot water."

"No, I didn't, but you can't drink that."

"Who says? I can do what I want."

"But…"

"NO BUTS!"

"Linda, leave it, Emma doesn't want to think about being pregnant or talk about it or anything." Mikela was trying to impress on her friend the need to leave the subject alone.

Luckily Linda was feeling happy and was more anxious to drink her beer than talk about babies, so she let it go.

They took a deep collective slug of beer and sighed with appreciation. Emma knew it would be her only one, it didn't taste quite right anyway, but she wasn't going to risk mentioning that. As their glasses knocked back down on the table, Chloe sauntered into the little scruffy bar. She was glowing too, the after effects of hot water, shampoo and sunshine giving her an amber halo.

"Wait for me, that looks so good, but Emma?"

"Just get your beer Chloe." Chloe picked up on the vibe and smiled winningly at the old man who seemed to double as barman. She came over with her glass and sat down gracefully.

"To us, sometimes it is the simple things in life that just make it all worthwhile. The four of us together, a functioning shower, a beer and a bed!"

"And fajitas, I'm starving." Mikela had sourced the nearest food before they had even booked into the hotel. Emma felt her stomach turn over at the thought of food, but she knew she had to eat something. She longed for her favourite meal of fresh goats' cheese salad and some crispy chips, but they would probably say she couldn't have that either. Dodgy fajitas would have to do. In the end that would be the last beer Emma drank, she just couldn't face it any more and the same went for coffee. Even if she didn't want to listen to her body, it was forcing her to.

Margot had been buoyed up by her conversation with Jan and she loved her gung-ho attitude, but she knew she had to take care. She didn't want to step over any lines any time soon with Jaime. If he had been someone more anonymous, someone less involved with her family, maybe she could have considered it. But she still loved Fred, the bastard. Paradoxically getting involved with any other man wouldn't have even occurred to her, but Jaime was almost part of the family and admittedly gorgeous. The evening she had spent with Fred before leaving had been like getting into a comfy warm bed on a winter's night, whereas flirting with Jaime and feeling his appreciation was very different and a bit risky. She would be wrong to play with his feelings though. What a mess she was, she was even still wearing her wedding ring, after all Fred had never said he wanted to leave her. But there it was again, the fact of what he had done, over and over again. She wanted to scream and rant and cry. She needed to live for the day as Fred had suggested. Maybe, being the nicely tanned gander that she was, she needed a little sauce to feel better about it all. But not with Jaime. Imagine the message to the kids as well if she started some kind of casual, non-permanent relationship with Jaime of all people, who her kids loved. She couldn't go off with somebody else though either, that would be awful all round. God her thinking was muddled. Damn you, Fred! Why couldn't you have resisted? But that was the answer really. She would resist, she would set the example and put her family first as usual.

Just then Rufus bounded in, heading straight for his water bowl followed by dishevelled looking Lucie.

"Hello boy, what have you been up to?"

"He is terrible, I've just had to pull him away from a horrible little chihuahua! He was trying to... you know... Honestly, I thought he was going to squash her to death. Her owner was going mental. And I thought he was in love with Lotta's dog."

"Oh dear!" Margot chuckled, "He can't really help it, Lucie. Is the owner still cross? Where were you?"

"It's OK, it was a couple down by the beach. The man kept yelling at his wife that he had told her she shouldn't have brought the dog to the beach when she is in heat and I managed to drag Rufus off. It was pretty embarrassing though."

"I can imagine."

"And pretty yucky!"

"Oh god, poor you!"

"Do you think it is the same with all males?" Lucie suddenly looked distressed and Margot's heart felt for her. She put her arm round her skinny shoulders and pulled her in for a hug.

"No Lucie, dogs are animals, they don't have a sense of morality or anything. They just follow their instinct. People are different." She hoped she sounded convincing, grateful to be talking into her daughter's hair and not looking her in the eyes.

"Yeah, well, maybe. Come here Rufus, you stupid old pooch." Rufus plumphed down next to Lucie on the old settee, liberally spraying her with his wet whiskers. He managed to look a little bit repentant. Lucie grabbed his ears and looked him squarely in the eyes.

"I still love you, you dafty, but pleeeease don't do that again."

Rufus whimpered lovingly and rubbed his sopping chin more firmly on her leg. Margot looked on, realising how intensely Lucie needed to see her dad and to believe in him again.

"You know what Lucie, when I spoke to Dad, he said he really wanted to come down and see us. He should be finished with his job soon. Shall I text him and tell him to come? Will Theo be all right with that do you think?"

"What if I tell Lotta how much I want Dad to come, she can work on Theo…"

"Lucie, Lucie, Lucie, guapita mia!" Uncle J had strolled into the kitchen in time to hear her last comment. "No need for manipulation my dear, not a pretty trait in a lady. Just you tell your brother straight, that is all it needs."

"I'm with Uncle J on this one. Let's not encourage any emotional blackmail or game-playing, let's all just try and be honest."

"Yep, no game-playing, that's good." Julian looked directly at Margot as right on cue, Jaime's scooter spluttered up to the terrace with a basket-full of foil wrapped kebabs. He jumped off his scooter and grabbed the kebabs.

"I have food, but I need beer!"

"There we are, direct and honest!" Uncle Julian winked at Margot and Lucie and headed for the fridge.

Fortunately, Jaime had one spare for Lotta and half an hour later the six of them were messily tucking into delicious, surprisingly lean, Donner kebabs. Faces and hands wiped, they decided to play Pictionary, the children's version. It was the only one they had anyway and also it made it easier for the different languages. Lotta and Theo couldn't be separated so Uncle J played on their team. It was a perfect evening and they laughed until their sides ached. Uncle J's drawing was hysterically bad and Jaime and Lotta were coming out with some hilariously wrong guesses. Theo was more relaxed than Margot could remember seeing him. He and little Lotta were so sweet and so happy in their loved-up cocoon. Margot suddenly realised how often she was touching Jaime, a playful punch here and a gentle tap on the arm there. It must stop. She was sending out all the wrong signals. Then suddenly they all got the giggles over a particularly bad drawing of a bull-dozer with horns and she relaxed again. As long as she was sure that things weren't going any further, it would be fine.

In fact, she was pretty transparent. Jaime knew more or

less where she was emotionally. He knew he would have to wait, or even better, do the decent thing and back off. Unfortunately, he just couldn't keep away. It was the whole thing, all of them, even the dog, but especially Margot. How anybody could have let her go he couldn't imagine. Although he had to admit that whereas she was glowing now, she had looked fragile before. That hadn't been a turn off for him in any way. He would have loved to have been in a position to protect her and cherish her. Maybe he was wrong, maybe it was him who was making her glow, maybe she was ready. He was kidding himself, he knew he had to hold off for now.

Chapter Fourteen

"That's it, lads! Done and dusted!" Fred held out his hand, shaking hands with each of the unlikely looking young men. They were all grinning with satisfaction. The weather was glorious, the grass had turned a summery green, the sun was reflecting on the shiny metal roof and sending back beams of light from the full-length window which looked over the valley. They had banged in the last nail and swept up the last sawdust the night before. That morning a group of notables had walked up to check out their work. The prison governor, a local member of parliament, the president of the CAF, a journalist and a photographer had come to appreciate and applaud their efforts. The lads were impressed, being congratulated and thanked was not something they were used to. Fred was proud, proud of the team and of himself, even of the prison governor for his imagination in setting up the project. But like a cloud coming over the sun, a shadow of gloom came over him. Would they have to go back to prison after all this? How would they be able to stand it?

The prison governor cleared his throat.

"Well done, all of you. You have all surpassed our expectations. You will be walking down the mountain tomorrow. At the bottom you will be met by a van, they will have your affairs and the papers you need to sign for your discharge. You will be taken to Briançon station and be given a train ticket to wherever you want to go and we will wish you all goodbye, good luck and a good trip!"

"Good riddance you mean!"

"Well, I definitely don't want to see you round my way again, that's for sure!"

It was a measure of everyone's improved psychological state that the mild joke was laughed at and a spontaneous applause was joined by all.

Soon after, Fred found himself pushing the door of his flat, feeling its gloom and emptiness. There was nothing for him there, he picked up his phone.

"Margot, hi, it's me…"

"Hey."

"Can I come and see the kids please, and you?"

"I said you could, of course."

"Tomorrow then. I'll drive down in the morning."

"Tomorrow? Um OK, um it's nearly the competition, but OK. Have you told Emma you're going to do that?"

"I haven't heard anything from Emma, so…"

Privately, Margot reflected that wasn't what she had asked but then again it wasn't her place to tell her husband, ex-husband, how to treat his girlfriend, mistress? Ah, she could feel herself bristling. Deep breaths.

"We'll be here. What time shall I tell the kids you'll be arriving?"

"What about a surprise? I don't know what time I'll get there anyway."

"OK, surprise it is."

Emma was feeling better, either she was learning how to pace herself or she'd got past the worst part of pregnancy already. She was fit and young after all, she didn't expect it to be too difficult. She had adapted her diet, easily given up coffee, alcohol and cream cheese. She was an athlete and she knew how to get her body into shape. And she'd borrowed a bra from Mikela which helped, even if she did have to wash it every night. But they had still only done one third of the trip, they were going to have to curtail it a bit.

"You know what? Maybe we should decide to aim for a shorter trip this time and we can finish the rest next year."

"What about, you know what?" Chloe pointed at Emma's belly.

"No, it's a great idea. Fred can look after it. It'll be just what I need, a break from it and to get back into shape."

The others glanced quickly at each other, they couldn't help it, but then who knew what Emma was capable of? They loved her for perpetually shocking them.

"Hopefully you won't still be saying 'it' by then."

"I wouldn't put it past her, but hey, let's go for it."

And so, they adjusted their plans and made a firm commitment to finishing their trip of a lifetime in a second instalment next summer.

"You know what? I think we'll enjoy it all the more now we've decided this."

"Maybe we can get a film crew to follow us when they see some of this trip."

"We need a few more Insta followers before that happens."

"Well Emma's new cleavage might help."

"Hey!"

"Joke, joke." Linda held up her hands in surrender. "It's not a bad idea though, a bit more exposed flesh might not be a bad thing. Or some cyclists' bums, close ups…"

"What? I teach in a school you know."

"So do I, don't worry, I can keep it tasteful."

"Oh my god, will you both shut up. We are thirty, not twenty and there is no way we are going down that road."

"Let's see, I'll try out some stuff and see what the reactions are and then you can all tell me what you think!"

"Let's just eat, shall we?" Emma was sober and hungry and fairly sure that Linda wasn't serious anyway. Mikela was easily distracted by her favourite subject.

"I love this food, I'm going to be so inspired when I get back to work."

"Mikela, you love all food, but I'm with you Emma, let's eat for goodness' sake." Chloe sounded distinctly irritated.

The next day, they were making good time, but Emma had the impression that Linda was behaving a bit strangely, dropping back unnecessarily or suddenly riding abreast, it was all a bit erratic.

"What on earth are you up to, L?"

"Nothing just trying things out, y'know."

"Hum, OK, if you say so."

Every day they picked a random spot on the map for their lunch break, they arrived early that day and were delighted by the beautiful riverside glade.

"Do you think it is safe to swim?"

"Course it is! Look at it, it is as clear as anything."

"No piranhas?"

"I don't think I'll risk it." Emma didn't feel like peeling off her sweaty stuff and then having to struggle back into damp things afterwards.

"Well, look the other way you guys. I'm going in." Chloe was already barefoot.

"Well, if you are, me too." Mikela was drawn to the pure green water.

Emma lay down in the shade under a tree, pulled her cap over her eyes and was instantly asleep.

Chloe and Mikela stripped off and were in the cool water in a flash, groaning with pleasure as their limbs floated to the surface. They eventually clambered out, grabbing their damp travel towels. Linda was nowhere to be seen, she'd probably gone for a little wander with a trowel and a loo roll. Emma was snoring quietly.

"So good! You don't often get the chance to swim like that do you, it just feels great."

"I know, I was still a bit worried someone might pass by, but it was worth it and we got away with it!"

"Emma was right about how horrible these sweaty things are to put back on though. Aah!"

"What the..." Emma sat up with a start to be greeted by the sight of Mikela half in and half out of her cycling shorts, sprawled across her legs.

"Oh my gosh, I wish I had that on film!" Chloe could hardly speak for laughing. Mikela had been trying to tug damp shorts over damp thighs and stepping backwards, she had tripped over Emma's feet and fallen flat on her back.

"Good grief, are you all right, Mikela?"

"I'm fine, just let me get these awful things back on in private!" Luckily, she had started laughing as well and there was no harm done.

"What's been going on here, rugby practice or some kind of strange yoga I've never heard of?" Linda arrived back, smiling.

"OK, enough, let's get back in the saddle, shall we? The water was lovely, thank you for asking, but you did have a point, Emma!"

"My power snooze was just great for me!"

"What about you Linda, a touch of the tourista?"

"Not at all, I just fancied some time on my own and to take few photos."

Mikela was fairly sure there was something not quite right with Linda, but she let it go.

Theo was ramping up his training. He couldn't believe how quickly his body was responding to it. He had to beg for some new t-shirts from his mum. Luckily, he was barefoot a lot of the time so he only needed one pair of skate shoes, because his feet were growing weekly. He had to borrow a wet-suit from Jaime, he couldn't squeeze himself into the old second-hand one any more. He felt great. He was shaving every day. His hands were either on the trapeze of a kite or Lotta. She was so cool, she made him laugh with her dry humour and then she would look at him with those sky-blue eyes as though he was the only thing in the world that existed. Her skin was velvety and he had very quickly and naturally learnt exactly what to do with his body and hers. He couldn't believe he had been worried about stuff like that before. The two of them were a couple and everyone on the beach knew that and it made him zing with pride. Getting well placed in the competition would be the perfect pinnacle of the perfect summer. He was living for the day and concentrating all his efforts on that, he would think about the future later. His mind just clamped down on the idea of returning to the sleazy, dull Lotta-less life he had before. Stop. He would sort it out after the competition.

It was Lucie who stayed most in touch with her friends from home. She hadn't found any girls of her age to hang out with and she was busy with Manté at lot of the time, so

Snapchat was enough extra social life for her. She also followed Emma's cycling Insta feed surreptitiously. For the last couple of days, she had noticed a change in the posts and stories coming from South America. Up until then it had all been pretty classic, cycling stuff, typical touristy snaps, the occasional picture of the group through the yellow bubbles of a cool glass of beer, but nothing special. There had been a couple of days with nothing posted at all and then, bang, a sudden flurry. And they were different. There was a fuzzy, soft-focus filter on most of the shots and a definite shift in style. There was no doubt that this was a bunch of fit young women cycling in extremely hot weather. The next day was even more obvious. There were bums, side boobs and sweaty cleavage galore. There weren't many films, Lucie supposed that filming while cycling was pretty difficult, but then suddenly there was a story. It started with a shot of the empty bikes, panned over to one of the girls sleeping in the shade and then moved over to two piles of clothes next to a river and then zoomed into the clear green water. And stopped. It felt weird to Lucie, but what did she care about what The Slut and her coven did for kicks. She shoved her phone in her pocket and jumped on her bike and pedalled for all she was worth in the direction of Manté and his golden sanity.

Manté blew lovingly down his nostrils at her and nuzzled his nose into the hollow of her shoulder. She hugged him fiercely before leading him out and leaping on his back. Forty-five minutes of intense work later, they were both sweaty, but happy. She led him to the water for a drink and then back to his cool stable to start brushing him down. She had given him a first stroke when her phone vibrated with a notification.

"It's The Slut again Manté, what now?" She clicked and

there were two or three seconds of naked bodies floating in pale green water. "You know what Manté, I don't think I need to do anything, that bitch is going to do it all for me." She put her phone away and concentrated on the task in hand as Manté whinnied his pleasure.

Chapter Fifteen

"Uncle J?"

"Yes, my bonny lass."

"Uncle J, Fred's coming." Margot was not sure what sort of reaction to expect from her loyal old uncle.

"Is he now, and what do you say to that?"

"I don't know really, I mean Lucie really misses him, so…"

"Do you miss him?"

"Well sort of, but that's neither here nor there really."

"Well, it is, but never mind. When is he arriving?"

"Sometime this afternoon, I think. I'm sorry it's such short notice."

"Well, we haven't got room for him here. I'll ask Rafa if his studio is free. It usually is, he can stay there."

Margot stepped towards her solid uncle and hugged him tight.

"That's perfect, a brilliant plan."

"Well, you know, I can be civil, but I can be Spanish too if you want. Just tip me the wink and he's dead meat. But on the other hand, I always did like Fred!"

"I know, me too, but what an idiot."

"You are too kind to him. Throwing away what he had is more than… but hey-ho, none of my business."

"The kids don't know yet, he wants it to be a surprise."

"I'm not sure how wise a surprise like that will be for Theo. And quite frankly Fred has forfeited the right to get what he wants. And this is my house, so I may have to have an extra little wander down to the beach. Rufus!"

Rufus gambolled over and the two of them were on their way out of the gate before Margot had had a chance to gather her thoughts.

"I'll speak to Rafa, don't worry."

"But…"

"No buts, my bonny lass, see you later!"

Margot sat down on the sun lounger, lent back and breathed out. Uncle J was right, Fred didn't get to decide any longer and it was them who would have to live with the consequences. Theo should be their first consideration and she needed a bit of shielding herself. She lay back, turning her face to the sun, feeling the dry heat warm through to her bones.

"Margot, hey!" Of course it was Jaime, of course it was.

"Hi Jaime, how are you?"

"Just checking on my star pupil."

"Theo is down at the beach already."

"Not Theo, as you well know. We need to look at nutrition for the next week. Up until now it has been fine, but you need to think a bit more carefully over the next few days."

"Oh god!"

"It's OK, nothing drastic, just a bit more pasta and salt to combat the dehydration, that kind of thing."

Margot sighed and ran her hand over her face.

"You don't like pasta? Sure you do, you love my gnocchi!" Jamie said with a wink.

Margot spluttered with laughter, "It's not that, Jaime."

"What is it then? No time for other stuff at the moment, the competition is in four days."

"Don't, you'll make me panic! No, the thing is…"

But the rest of her sentence was drowned out by wheels on gravel and a car door slamming. Fred appeared on the terrace. He was looking tanned and comfortable, if slightly car worn.

"Fred!"

"Margot! You look fantastic!"

Margot had jumped to her feet and stepped towards the road. Jaime took it all in, turned and left by the gate from the terrace. "See you later Margot, we'll sort it out tomorrow."

"Who was that?" Fred's interest was piqued, his beautiful wife was standing in front of him in a dusty pink bikini top and bleached cut off denims. She was hazelnut brown and her hair was wild and streaked with light copper, held back off her face with sunglasses. She was barefoot and stunning and the guy who was striding athletically away matched her in colour and surf style.

"Jaime is the kite-surf instructor, it's his club."

"Oh yes, you mentioned him." Fred let the feeling go.

"Can I get you a beer?"

"Fantastic, can I have a glass of water first do you think? Where is everybody?"

"Don't forget you wanted to surprise them." Margot was getting irritated, he couldn't get to play the returning hero, or expect her to wait on him.

"Lucie is at the stables and Uncle J and Theo are at the beach with Rufus. Julian was going to ask Rafa if his studio is free for you to stay in." Fred looked crestfallen, which was irritating too.

"Fred, you can't walk into our lives just like that. And there's no room for you here. Did you think we could share a room or something?"

Fred held his hands out pleadingly.

"I'm sorry Margot, I was just so excited to see you all."

And because she knew him so well, she knew it was true, there was no harm meant, no mega-ego at work, it was just Fred being transparent.

"OK, OK, well what if we went over to see Lucie, she'll be so happy, she is dying for you to meet Manté. Short for Mantequilla, by the way."

"I know, I know, she told me! Margot, that would be the best thing in the world." His sincerity and knowing how delighted Lucie would be at the surprise, won her over.

"Come on then, a beer goes down pretty quickly in this heat anyway, I'll take you over."

"Margot, thank you, really." He stepped towards a hug, but they both froze before it could happen.

A quick fifteen minutes later and they were pulling into the white gravelled courtyard in front of a traditional straw-coloured hacienda. The stables flanked one side and on the other was a dusty red manège surrounded by simple fencing. Fred uncurled himself from the car.

"She's over there, look. And that's Manté."

Lucie was leading Manté from the other side of the ring. She had a white T-shirt and traditional jodhpurs with short beige boots. Her hair was swinging in a long blond pony-tail, her face and arms were nut brown. She was leading her horse by the reins, but stroking his cheek with the other hand. It was obvious from the twitching of his ears that she was whispering sweet nothings to him. Fred's heart thumped hard, his beautiful little girl was growing up and he hadn't been on hand to see. He stood and watched as they made their way to the edge of the car-park. Suddenly Manté whinnied and Lucie looked up and saw him.

"Dad, Dad!" She couldn't run into his arms because she couldn't leave go of Manté, but he could run to her.

"Lucie, Lucie, Lucie Loo. Hey, Manté!" He grabbed her with both arms in a massive bear hug, lifting her off the ground, but he could still pat the curious, but patient horse.

"He's lovely, aren't you, old fella?"

Manté looked almost coy, he could tell this man was important to Lucie and Lucie was very important to him.

"Mum, you didn't tell me."

"He wanted to surprise you Lucie, Theo doesn't know yet either."

"Oh Dad, it's great to see you."

"And you Lucie, you look fantastic, more and more like your mum. Apart from your hair, you've gone so blond."

"I have to put Manté away, you can help if you like."

"I can't think of anything I'd rather do."

Margot chuckled, she knew that Fred was really not that keen on horses, especially in closed spaces, but then again who knew? What did she really know about him these days? Thirty minutes later, they were on their way home. Lucie left her bike at the stables with Fred promising her a lift back the next day. It all felt so normal.

"I can't wait to see you ride, Lucie!"

Lucie was beaming with pride and the sheer joy of having her mum and dad in the same car.

"What about Theo? What's he going to say?" Lucie suddenly looked worried.

"Uncle J went to warn him, don't worry, he'll be fine."

Fred looked chastened again.

"It'll be fine Fred, he's changed."

"And he's in love!" Lucie chipped in.

"In love?"

"Yes, with Lotta, they are really, really soppy…" Lucie stuck two fingers down her throat to indicate how she felt about her brother's PDAs with his girlfriend. Margot and Fred both laughed, Fred automatically patted Margot's hand on the gear-stick. She shook her head and shifted gear. He pulled his hand away sheepishly.

"Sorry, habit." Right, so that was irritating again, but then Margot felt Fred tense up as they arrived at the house and felt sorry for him again. It was hard to see him so nervous about seeing his own son. They climbed out of the car and Fred was immediately pushed backwards as Rufus bounded towards him, jumping up to give his beloved master a big slobbery kiss with his paws firmly pinning him back against the car door.

"Good grief Rufus, get down, you daft old hound!" He brushed off some sand and slobber and crouched down to give his loyal friend the hug he deserved. "Ah, Rufus, have you been good?"

"He's been so good, Dad, apart from when he tried to diddle that horrible rat down the road."

"He tried what?"

Margot laughed, glad the tension had eased a bit, "A story for later, come this way."

With all the kerfuffle, Uncle J and Theo were standing on the edge of the terrace waiting for them. Fred stepped forward with his hand held out, Uncle J grabbed it and shook it hard, his other hand clasping Fred's shoulder. It wasn't quite the hug of yore, but it was welcoming.

"Looking well, Fred."

"You too, Uncle J, you're looking very dapper. Theo…"

He held out his hand again and when Theo took it, he pulled him into a massive and inescapable hug. Theo resisted, but then gave in and let himself be momentarily held by the dad he missed to his very core, but then he pushed him away.

"Dad!" He was guarded but he was talking to him, Fred would take that.

"Well, you lot, grab a seat and I'll get some drinks. Give me a hand Theo, will you?" Uncle J diffused the situation with tact and that particular 'seen it all before, you won't ruffle me' wisdom that comes with age. Lucie pulled off her hot riding boots and sank into the settee.

"Sit here, Dad. Rufus, come here."

Rufus didn't need asking twice, he spread himself firmly on top of Fred and Lucie, pinning them in place. Margot needed to move, she headed for the sanctuary of the cool kitchen to help the other two. She had just ducked into the shady interior when she heard a welcoming yap from Rufus. She hoped it wasn't Jaime again.

"The-o! It's Lot-ta!" Lucie shouted for her brother with the glee of a mocking younger sister.

Theo loped out and straight to where Lotta was entering the garden. He pulled her to his side with one arm round her shoulder and a quick kiss hello. Lotta reached up and brushed his hair to one side and then dropped her hand to his stomach. They looked every bit a couple, Fred looked on in amazement. In a few short weeks his stringy, spotty little lad had metamorphosed into a man, a surf dude and a lover by the looks of things. Lotta was lovely, sure she was young, but she didn't look like a kid either. Fred closed his gaping mouth and struggled to pull himself out of the low soft settee, to the displeasure of Rufus.

"Get off, you great lump!" Eventually he managed to squirm out from under the big pile of sandy fur and haul himself upright. He stepped towards Theo and Lotta.

"Dad, this is Lotta. Lotta, my dad."

Fred leant forward and kissed Lotta on both cheeks.

"Hello Lotta, it's really lovely to meet you. What can I say? Just wow!"

"Dad, sit down." Theo had a slightly warning note in his tone. "Let's have a drink. Coke, Lotta? Orangina, brat?" Lucie threw a cushion at her brother who caught it deftly and lobbed it back straight on her head.

"Oy!"

"Kids!" Margot and Julian were making their way back out to the terrace with trays of wine, drinks, ice cubes, thin crisps, fat olives and delicious squares of cold tortilla. It looked familiar and refreshing and, as far as Fred was concerned, more than he could ever have hoped for.

"Did you have a good drive, Fred?"

"Not bad at all Uncle J, I set off really early, so there was no traffic at all until about nine, so all good!"

"I got Rafa's studio for you, did Margot say? Do you remember where it is?"

"Not exactly, over on the main road down towards the beach I think."

"Exactly, there's no parking, but you can leave your car here."

"That's really kind. Thanks." Fred was suddenly conscious that Julian was being extremely gracious and generous. For a brief moment whilst enjoying the pleasures of being with his family, he had forgotten that he had no rights any longer, he had forfeited them. His expression was completely transparent and both Margot and Julian jumped in to stop him getting too serious, too soon.

"Did you know Fred, that it is only four days until the big competition?"

"Can you stay for that, Dad?" Theo suddenly sounded like a little boy again, in spite of the beautiful girl at his side and his shoulders to rival an American footballer.

"Hey, I'm on holiday mate and nothing would keep me from watching you race."

"And Mum."

"I know, I can't believe it, your mum in a kite-surf race."

"Hey, she's really good." Lucie was bristling as a vision of the wretchedly sporty Slut swam in front of her eyes.

"I'm sure she is, she's always been really quick at picking up new sports. I remember the first time we went hydro-speeding, you just loved it didn't you, Margot?"

"That's true, gosh, that was a long time ago. I was pretty good at that, wasn't I?"

"You must be a natural at water sports, bonny lass." Uncle J was reassuring and calm. Lucie relaxed, nobody had actually mentioned T.S. to be fair.

"Do you kite-surf, Lotta?" Fred asked.

"A little bit, actually I prefer wind-surfing, I don't know why."

Theo smiled at her. "She is pretty good at both!"

"Your English is excellent, Lotta."

"Thank you, it is easy to learn when you live in Holland;"

"And you have an English boyfriend." Lucie was hoping to tease, but Lotta wasn't in the least fazed.

"That's true, it is really good way of progressing." Theo leant over and kissed her. Lucie made throwing up noises and

Theo grabbed one of the many cushions lying around and threw it like a Frisbee at his sister.

"Hoy!"

"Hoy yourself!"

"Hey both of you, poor Lotta getting in the middle of you two." Margot was laughing though, it all felt so right.

"You know what, I didn't tell you all yet, because I wasn't sure, but I am going to be riding Manté in Thursday night's show. You can all come and watch!"

"No way!" "Fantastic!" "Great news! "Lucie!" They were all suitably impressed. Lucie buffed her nails on her imaginary lapels.

"It's great timing, Manté is on super form."

"That is so lucky, Lucie Loo, I am so lucky to be here to see your first display."

Lucie bristled again, thinking that if he hadn't been so stupid, he would have automatically been there, but they were all so happy and she didn't want to be the one to spoil Dad's arrival. She wasn't the only one to have had the thought though and a slight shift fell over the gathering.

"So come on, Fred, I'll show you Rafa's place while this lot get some food organised. Whose turn is it?" Uncle J was on his feet, dangling a set of keys before anyone could say what they were thinking.

"It's mine," said Lucie.

"Tell you what, Lucie, I'll give you a hand, if you help me tomorrow. Your dad will have to step up to the plate too." Margot didn't want her little girl brooding on her own in the dark kitchen.

"What's this?" Fred was curious.

"Dinner rota, Dad, number one rule, no complaining!"

Theo laughed at his dad's crestfallen face.

"Is there still that little bistro round the corner?"

"It's still there."

"Sorted!"

"Dad! That's cheating!"

"What did you just say rule number one is?"

"True, true, and I'm not complaining if I don't have to eat your cooking."

"Hey!"

Chapter Sixteen

"Have you seen how many likes we're getting on Instagram?" Mikela was looking at her phone in amazement. It was the first time in a few days that they had had some Wi-Fi and her phone had been beeping wildly before she could turn the sound down.

"Actually, I haven't looked yet." Emma was staying uncharacteristically away from social media. She didn't want to have too much contact with Fred. She was still quite worried about what his reaction to her news was going to be if she let herself think about it. She had decided to firmly live for the day. The trip was turning out to be as glorious as she had always hoped it would be. The people were so friendly and forthcoming, the surrounding countryside was stunning and she could easily cope with the slightly reduced pace they were doing now. She was living in a multi-coloured Hispanic bubble and loving it. She had even stopped feeling sick.

"What's Linda been posting then?"

"I'm just lo…Oh no, WHAT?"

"What is it, Mikela?"

"She's turned us into a porn site!"

"What? How? We've all been behaving like nuns!"

"Well, a pregnant nun in your case! Look for yourself, it's horrible…"

Emma was already scrolling as Mikela continued exclaiming.

"What has she done? Oh Mikela, I didn't know you and

Chloe swam in the nude!"

"Look at this one of your bum, it's obscene!"

"Thanks a lot, at least it's covered up and anonymous."

"You know what I mean, not your bum, but the fact that she posted it. Look at this one of Chloe's side boob. When did she even take these?"

"That's why she has been riding so erratically."

"Mikela, Emma, have you seen this?" Chloe was red-faced and out of breath.

"Just now, what's the matter with her?"

"She's lost the plot, she wants to be a reality star or something and this is how she thinks she can do it."

"It's so crass, I can't believe it."

"God knows what my sponsors will say." Chloe looked really worried.

"And my bosses, they were really good to us."

"And Fred." The other two grimaced in sympathy.

"I want to kill her — slowly. Where is she anyway?" Mikela was uncharacteristically angry, but she was also extremely self-conscious about her body and the thought of being exposed online to all and sundry, was more than she could bear.

"I saw her heading out of the hotel, all dolled up." Chloe was still scrolling and zooming, her head shaking continuously.

"She'll be out on the make, she can't go too long without some action."

"Hopefully, she won't film that and put it out there." Emma sounded bitter.

"Friends, eh?"

"Look, let's limit the problem, we can take all this lot down and hope not too many people have seen it. It's only been there for a couple of hours presumably." Emma was pretending to be the voice of reason, realising that her friends were panicking, even though seeing the numbers going steadily up she knew it was pretty much in vain. "Let me get to it."

"And I'll go and find Linda and personally..." Mikela was still raging.

"Emma is right." Chloe was calming down, "Let's have a drink, Mikela, maybe it'll all be OK."

Linda didn't get back until the others had all been asleep for hours. By then Emma had taken down the photos and posted a classic photo of their dusty, panier-laden bikes in front of the hotel and a view of the scenery behind it. They had also added a great shot that Mikela had taken of a particularly spectacular sunset a couple of days previously. Then they had a lucky break, Chloe managed to film a devastatingly cute kitten on the terrace of the hotel which had chased a green lizard into a hole in a wall. The lizard kept popping his head out and every time the kitten would jump back in fright before remembering who was supposed to be the hunter.

"Brilliant Chloe, there's nothing like kittens for getting likes."

"Well, you know nude women would normally do the job too right?" Chloe had taken positive steps to try and limit the damage Linda had done, but she was still seething with rage. It was lucky that Linda had stayed out. Emma was still keeping one eye on her phone, keeping check of the situation.

"Oh no!"

"What?" Mikela was slumped over her beer and was not at all sure she could handle any more trauma.

"There's one of my students. I recognise his pseudo. Jeez,

what does that even mean?"

"It means they fancied you before and now they've seen even more of you than they ever hoped. Their imaginations must be rampant." Mikela was past trying to cheer anybody else up.

"Let's just forget it, pretend it happened to somebody else." Chloe was trying to be upbeat.

"Like the virtual equivalent of today's news being tomorrow's fish and chip paper, you mean? With my luck there would be a big photo of my boobs floating to the surface on the outside of every cone. Schoolboys up and down the country pouring ketchup on my nipples…"

Chloe and Emma burst out laughing, even at her lowest Mikela could always be counted on to make them laugh.

In St Pere Pescador, Lucie was struggling to get to sleep. She was so excited about her dad being there to see her and Manté do their first display. She picked up her phone and started automatically scrolling through her updates. There wasn't much new, one of her friends had posted a new TikTok routine she would have to start practising, another had posted yet more heart invested pink filtered photos of Noah Centineo, could she not just move on? Suddenly there were the photos she had seen before of The Slut and her cronies, the bizarre close-ups and even some full-frontal nudity. She'd forgotten about them in her excitement at Dad turning up, but now she had to talk to somebody about it, she would never get to sleep otherwise.

"Theo, Theo, are you awake?" She had crept along the creaky landing and was shaking her brother's shoulder.

"No." Theo turned his back to his sister.

"Yes, you are, look at this…"

Theo turned over grumpily, glaring at his sister and squinting at the phone she was thrusting towards his nose.

"What is it? Why are you showing me that? You haven't woken me up to show me pictures of kittens, have you? Have you gone completely loopy?" Struggling up through the clouds of sleep, Theo was curious, he couldn't remember the last time his little sister had woken him up in the middle of the night.

"No, look, it's The Slut and her cronies naked!"

"What!" Theo was sitting up, completely awake. "What are you on about? Where?"

"Look, you dope!" Lucie grabbed her phone back, but then looked confused. "That's weird, they've gone!"

"What have?"

"There were all these sleazy close-ups of their bums and boobs and some of them swimming naked in green slime. It was horrible."

"Maybe you were dreaming?"

"No look, the comments are still there. That one is from one of the boys I know who goes to Dad's school."

Theo reached for his own phone and started looking more closely.

"Hmm, they must have been taken down… Listen Luce, don't say anything to anyone. Everything feels good, so much better, let's just keep this quiet. Nobody needs to know for now." He held up his fist to his little sister, inviting a concluding bump. Lucie felt like she had suddenly grown up, she knew what he meant and she bumped his fist with a smile.

"You're right Theo, glad you didn't see them anyway!" She grinned naughtily at her big brother, she knew about his crush after the tree-park day.

"Right, that's it, go to bed, squirt, we'll check it all out in the morning."

"OK, OK, night bruv." She would sleep now, she had passed on the worry.

Theo rolled on his back and stared into the darkness. He had seen how happy his dad was to be back with them all. He wasn't sure how to read his mum's reactions, but she hadn't looked sad or angry. Maybe they could all go back to the way things were. He prodded his own hurt, he wasn't really angry in the same way as before. Then, there had been an all-encompassing black rage, but now he felt almost sorry for his dad. He was so happy with Lotta that he had no desire to hold on to all the negative feelings. He wanted to shout out his feelings for her and for everybody around him to be doused in happy rainbow colours. Good grief! He pushed further and acknowledged that he had over-reacted, well perhaps not over-reacted because it had been all wrong, but he had reacted from his gut without thinking because he had been in such a bad place himself. So if his mum could seem to be happy and civil, so could he. And if Emma, or TS, as Lucie called her, was involved in dodgy stuff with explicit photos online, then surely his dad wouldn't want her back. And once he had seen Mum in the competition, he'd be under her spell again. To be honest he had looked pretty smitten with her all day.

Fred fell asleep the moment his head hit the pillow. He jerked awake in the middle of the night not knowing where he was. He lay back down on the extremely comfortable bed, relaxing after six weeks in a small cramped tent. What a day it had been. He felt lighter. as though he had shed a heavy rucksack after a long arduous climb. His family had been happy to see him, all of them. He would give anything just to stay, he would have to take it easy, one day at a time.

Chapter Seventeen

The girls had established a standard departure time early in the trip. They all had different routines in the morning from half an hour's stretching, to leaping from bed ten minutes before leaving and doing up shoes with an apple in the mouth. That morning, Emma, Chloe and Mikela were ready and waiting when Linda stumbled towards them looking messed up and ill. The others looked at her dispassionately.

"Ready? Let's go." Chloe's expression was fixed and determined.

They set off with Linda still scrambling to get herself together. None of them had seen her since their discoveries the night before and looking at the smudged make-up lurking round her eyes, she hadn't been back long. They cycled solidly for two hours. Emma and Mikela set the pace and Chloe settled in behind them with her earphones firmly in place. Linda finally managed to get the rhythm after half-an-hour of flailing about and groaning. It was time for a break and they had just reached the top of a steady climb. The view across the wide, flat valley and the mountains in the distance was breathtaking. They pulled off their helmets and grabbed their ground-sheets. They had quickly realised that lying on the ground without protection was a no-no. There were way too many curious insects and spiky grass pods. As they sat down and then laid back, Linda had the impression she was crawling towards them on her knees, begging forgiveness. Nobody had really spoken all morning.

"Food, Linda?" Mikela was mad at her, but she was still her friend and she looked awful. Linda grabbed the olive branch disguised as a sandwich.

"Thank you so much, Mik."

"So what did you get up to last night?" Emma felt vaguely jealous, she and Linda had always been the wild ones.

Linda lay back with a sigh,

"Actually, I'm not sure. Last thing I remember, I was dancing with this gorgeous guy."

"Beer bottle specs, perchance?"

"I don't think so, these Latinos are pretty hot. Anyway, I zapped a few hours and then I found myself on a swing on the front porch of a little house not far from the hotel. I had a blanket over me and it was daylight. I recognized the road and hot-footed it back. Great night really."

"God, Linda." Chloe looked disgusted. "You'll... No, never mind. It's your choice."

"Yes, but what isn't your choice is to put those photos online, Linda." Emma was not going to let her get away with anything just because of a hang-over or potential date rape.

"Poor Mikela was in bits."

"What? Why? Did you see how many followers we have now?"

"Linda, we are not all in the same place as you on that, you can post what you like of yourself, on your own post, but don't drag us all down to your level." Chloe knew she sounded priggish, but frankly she was sick of her friend behaving like a naive teenager.

"Yeah, frankly Linda, you stepped over the line on this one." Emma was getting angry again. Mikela was holding herself and reliving the horrors of the world looking at her naked body. "Look at Mikela, she didn't ask to feel like that."

"I don't get it, what are you on about? There was nothing out of order."

"Sure, never mind, let's leave it for now. We're in the middle of nowhere and we've got to keep it together."

"But…" Linda was going to justify herself again but she could see from their faces that it wasn't going to help.

They finished eating in silence. The only shade was the small amount they could get from their bikes, so they laid in a line looking at the spectacular view. Then Linda started to snore.

"Geez, it just gets better." Mikela had her elbow raised ready to nudge her worse-for-wear friend.

"Leave her, we've got more chance of all getting there today if we let her recover a bit." Emma didn't want any more arguments, she knew that her pregnancy had already put a strain on the group and she wasn't sure how much more they could handle.

An hour later, they were back in the saddle.

"You know, I don't think I did anything last night, I'm not chaffing at all." Linda sounded almost disappointed.

"Yuck! That is so bad! Do you often sleep with somebody and not be able to remember it?" Mikela sounded horrified.

"Well how would I know if I can't remember. Anyway, who cares? You know it's just like scratching your nose or taking a shower, right?"

"Good grief, is that what you really think?" Mikela was looking horrified now.

"You haven't been doing it right Linda, in that case." Chloe's dry comment had them all laughing.

"And don't forget that we used to share a flat with you and we know about you and the shower!" Emma spluttered and the tension eased.

An hour and a half later, they were nearing their destination. Linda was exhausted, the effect of the night before combined with a pretty hilly day and a particularly hot sun were really making themselves felt. She yawned and took her eyes off the road and that was all it took. She hit a rock which spun her so that her front wheel clipped the back of Emma's bike. She wrenched the handlebars and fell flat on her side pulling her bike on top of her. She felt her wrist crunch as she went down on it. Emma wobbled and fell in slow motion. Mikela was screaming.

"I'm OK, Mikela, don't worry." Emma stood straight back up dusting herself off.

"But the baby!"

"It'll be fine, I didn't go down hard."

Linda didn't stand up so fast. Chloe ran to her side.

"Stay still, keep your head down. I think you've properly injured your wrist. It doesn't look great."

Linda groaned, turned her head and vomited. Chloe leapt back and grabbed her phone.

"God, we're going to need help. What do we do now?" Mikela was looking terrified.

"Can you stop a car?" Emma decided she had better sit down again. "When did we see the last one?"

"Look, quick! There's one, come on, Mikela." Chloe grabbed her hand. Their distress, crashed bikes and two girls on the ground meant that the driver of the car took pity on them.

A harrowing six hours later found them gratefully sitting in the bar of a small hotel. Linda was sporting a full arm plaster and grinning soporifically as the South American painkillers took effect. The hotelier bought them some tacos and jugs of lemonade. None of them could face alcohol.

"So time to go home, how are we going to do it?" Mikela had had enough adventure. As usual Chloe was organised.

"It's OK, the insurance company pays for us all to go back in the circumstances. It's a good job we took that slightly more expensive cover."

"I'll never complain again." Emma hugged her efficient friend. "Thanks Chloe, I don't think I could happily carry on now."

"No way!" Mikela was looking horrified again. "We need to get you home."

"Exactly, you were lucky Emma, it could have been much worse. As it is, we'll all be home by tomorrow night, late, but we'll be back."

They sighed collectively, relief mingled with disappointment, but after the day they'd had, the relief was coming out on top.

"Anyway, we've already decided to continue next year!" Emma smiled and raised her glass. "To next year!"

Chapter Eighteen

The equestrian display was superb. None of them, with exception of Julian, had much idea what to expect, but they were all thrilled. Lucie and Manté were with five other horses and their riders and they were all throbbing with perfect synchronisation. The fiery Spanish music fitted perfectly. The costumes were minimal, simple black t-shirts and jodhpurs, but the effect of the blond horses with their manes and tails plaited with black ribbon was striking. Lucie had been surprisingly calm beforehand as her mum plaited black ribbons into her own hair.

"Aren't you nervous?" Her brother was secretly impressed by her lack of jitters.

"No, I can't wait!" Lucie's absolute confidence shone through.

As the show finished, Fred had tears in his eyes, he caught Margot's eye over Julian's head, she smiled sheepishly at him as she wiped a tear away. Afterwards Lucie ran up to them and Uncle Julian grabbed hold of her first.

"Fantastic, Lucie, brilliant!"

"I know, did you see how perfect he was?"

"You too, my guapita."

"I just sat there, Uncle J, Manté did it all."

Fred and Margot hugged her with pride.

"I don't think it would have been the same with me on his back Lucie Loo!"

"If Theo and I do half as well tomorrow, we'll be happy!"

"Oh Mum, you will and it's great you're here, Dad!" Lucie kissed him on the cheek and he realised how very long it had been since she had done that last.

"Right, one glass of sangria each and I'm taking you all home. Tomorrow is another big day!" Julian waved the keys of his old beach jeep with intent.

The next morning the weather looked right. Uncle J wandered down to the beach to have a quick paddle, but Jaime was stressing so much that he decided to give it a miss and have a coffee at Lotta's mum's place instead.

"Can you spare a coffee for an old man, my dear? Even if you are not really open yet?"

"You're not competing this afternoon then Julian?" Lotta's mum smiled at him.

"No categories for the over eighties apparently, insurance problems!"

"Shame on them! Lotta is really nervous for Theo, I heard her tossing and turning all night."

"Well, I think it is a pretty big deal for them, my dear! Be warned!" He picked up his cup and winked at her. "You and I both know that there is no perfect recipe for happiness, so good luck to the two of them I say!"

Lotta's mum came round the counter and gave Julian a hug, she clinked her coffee cup with his.

"Here's to happiness, whenever it happens."

"Here's to that." Julian caught sight of her involuntary glance towards Jaime as he buzzed about, preparing the biggest day of the year for his club.

At the villa, Theo and Margot were eating scrambled eggs on toast, with fruit smoothies. According to Jaime it was the breakfast of champions. They were nearly finished when Fred turned up.

"Any chance of a coffee?"

"Sure, but you'll have to get your own. Theo and I are not allowed coffee this morning."

"You drink coffee now, Theo?"

"Course, Dad." Theo's expression said it all.

"Of course you do. I've got so much catching up to do."

"Well, no time this morning, Mum and I have got some stretching to do. Ready, Mum?"

"Give me five minutes, I need a yoghurt to settle my tummy." Margot grimaced.

"Don't be nervous, you're bound to be fine. I'll go and start warming up." Theo's enthusiasm meant that Margot really had no choice but to try and keep up with him.

"Wow, this is really important for him, isn't it?"

"It really is, but don't worry, he's good and he has worked hard. Don't expect him to win, but he will do well."

"And you?"

"I get a point for the club if I compete, so no pressure for me. It's really just for fun at my age."

"This is me you're talking to Margot, don't try and tell me you don't care about winning. I've played Scrabble with you!"

She smiled and bashed the back of his hand with her teaspoon.

"Well maybe, anyhow first I have to go and stretch with that son of ours."

"See you later then and good luck."

Fred watched wistfully, as his lovely wife wandered off to join his all grown up son.

He was still sitting on the terrace staring out at the sea

when Lucie came up behind him and put her arms round him like she used to.

"Lucie Loo, how are you?" The sing-song refrain of her childhood made her tighten her hug. "You were a superstar last night. Can we watch the race together later?"

"Course, we'd better leave Rufus here though, he might do something daft, like that other time."

"He'll be all right with me if he's on the lead."

And that was true, which made Lucie smile even more. Things were really getting back to normal.

Whilst Lucie went to shower, Fred finally managed to work the coffee machine. He was trying not to think, just enjoy his surroundings when his phone beeped. Having turned off most of his notifications it was a fairly rare occurrence. He felt his stomach twist as he slid a reluctant thumb over the screen.

"Hey babe, where are you? The house looks empty. That's right, I'm back. Long story, big news. See you later XOXOX"

He dropped the phone with a clatter. Emma was home, she wasn't due back for another six weeks. What was the news? She had hardly been in touch since she left, and now she had news? What would she say if she knew where he was? Did he care? What now? He wished he could unread the message. Well, he wasn't going to answer it now, it would have to wait until after the competition.

"Hey, Dad, shall we go for a swim? It'll be too busy later I think."

"Great idea, can I borrow a towel?"

"No problem, let's go."

It wasn't a difficult decision.

Emma had been surprised not to find Fred at home waiting for her, but she realised that he was hardly going to be just sitting around all summer. There was a dirty coffee cup in the sink so he'd probably just gone for a hike. She texted him, knowing he wouldn't have his phone switched on if he was in the mountains. Hopefully he would pick it up when he stopped for lunch. Suddenly she felt quite anxious about his reactions. She had managed to put the whole situation out of her head, but faced with the imminent prospect of telling Fred he was going to be a father again, the realities of having a baby crowded in on her. All those things Mikela had mentioned, crèche, holidays, lack of freedom, getting huge, even pushing the thing out, for goodness' sake. She looked down at herself, at her narrow hips and slightly bulging tummy. For the moment she just looked like she had eaten a big lunch, but soon it would kick off. She stroked the curve. She did want this baby, but she really hoped she wouldn't have to do it on her own. Financially that would be tough. When would she ever get a break from it and do some stuff in the mountains? She had to get Fred on board, she regretted not having contacted him more while she had been away. She ran distraught fingers through her hair. It had grown back in and was quite a nice streaky blond from the sun, but it could definitely do with some re-styling. 'Keep focussed Em, you know how to keep your man interested.' She picked up her phone and cajoled her hairdresser into giving her an appointment that afternoon.

By the end of the afternoon, Julian, Fred, Lucie and Lotta were wrung out. It had been exciting and exhilarating, but also incredibly nerve-wracking. Lotta's mum had taken pity on a frantic Rufus and shut him behind her cool bar with a bowl of water.

"Wow, I'm going to be all bruised from you grabbing me,

Lucie!" Fred was rubbing his biceps.

Lucie and Lotta were still jumping up and down, unable to keep still. Theo had come fourth which was absolutely unheard of for a rookie competitor. And Margot had come second! Admittedly the field had been small, but it was still an amazing feat.

The prize-giving was about to take place. The competitors were out of their wetsuits, but they were still separated from the public. Margot was waiting, grinning from ear to ear, Jaime grabbed her for a massive hug.

"You killed it babe!" And she felt like a babe as she hugged him back.

"All thanks to you, Jaime." She didn't linger in his arms, she could see her family over his shoulder. She bounded up onto the podium waving madly at them. Fred had seen the hug, but he waved and whistled as madly as the others.

Theo slipped under the separating rope and grabbed Lotta.

"No prize for being fourth!'

"Don't be daft, you did fantastically well." Lotta had leapt onto him and he was twirling her round. The others crowded round, back-slapping and clapping. It was the perfect family moment. But then Fred's phone started vibrating, bringing him back to earth with a thump. Even if he wanted to just stay, it wasn't up to him. He looked over at Margot, she was radiating joie-de-vivre, maybe because he wasn't in her life any more.

"Er, I'm just going to check on Rufus." He edged away from his whooping family and listened to the message on his phone. Apparently, it was vital for him to hurry home. It was really, even if it was only to finish things with Emma. He couldn't expect Margot to even consider taking him back if he was still involved with someone else. He was going to drive back now and sort things out. He too had important news.

"Lucie, I'm going to have to go back, I'm sorry. I'll be back soon."

"Now? Can't you stay for tonight?"

"You know I really want to, you know that. But I really can't. Will you explain to the others? I don't want to make a fuss now."

"Oh Dad." Lucie put her arms round his waist and sighed. "OK, but promise you'll be back?"

"I promise, I love it here with you guys."

Lucie had grown up a lot in the last few months and she knew she had to not make a fuss. "OK, if you promise, I'll tell them later."

"Bye Luce, look after Rufus."

Leaving the keys for the studio on the table and grabbing a bottle of water, he was on his way. All he wanted to do was celebrate the fantastic afternoon with his family, but sorting out the rest of his life was pretty high on his list of priorities as well.

"Where's Dad, Lucie?"

"He had to go suddenly, but he promised he'd be back."

Margot sighed, she'd been getting used to having Fred back, but if he couldn't even stay for this celebration, what was the point? A loud pop interrupted her thoughts as Jaime opened a bottle of cava.

"A drink to toast your successes and for once I'll let you off wetsuit duty!"

"Thanks Jaime, here's to your superb organisation and for making me do it! I loved it!" Margot clinked glasses with Jaime and kissed him on the cheek. He held her regard for a second too long, but continued on to fill up the next glass.

"Cheers my dear, you did me proud!"

"Thanks Uncle J. Did you see Theo though?"

"He's a lad who has found his way, I don't think we'll have to worry about him too much any more!"

Margot looked over to where Theo had one arm around Lotta while he slapped the shoulder of the other super cool surfers the place was filled with.

"You could be right!" She smiled.

Fred drove determinedly, but carefully. He felt a weight had lifted from him. After all Emma had left him for weeks without a second thought. It was a new school year coming up. It was time for new beginnings. Emma would just have to understand that his children came first. He turned the Foo Fighters up loud and sang along.

Chapter Nineteen

It was September, a new term. It was the first of same old interminable meetings around the same old table which still gave him cold sweats. Emma was folding lotus flowers, Fred was staring at his pencil case. The irony.

Emma had been able to adjust the terms of her sabbatical and had come back to work. Everyone knew she was expecting Fred's baby, she hadn't seen any reason to keep it quiet and it had stopped them commenting on her super short hair. Bernie slapped his old mate on the shoulder and bent his head close to his.

"I heard great things about your job with the lads!"

"You were right, it's a good scheme. It definitely made a difference to them. I'm not sure I exactly enjoyed it, but it was worth it."

"And now this! Congratulations!" The words were fine, but Bernie's expression was questioning.

Fred grimaced, "If only you knew."

"Actually, Sophie was talking to Margot, and I think maybe I do know a little bit."

Fred nodded with a sigh, "Can we grab a beer later?"

"We can and indeed must, me old pal." Bernie patted his shoulder again and moved on round the table.

At the end of the day, they wandered off to the least popular bar in town. The beer was not too bad, you just had to ignore the deco and dust which had not been disturbed since the early seventies.

"What are you going to do, Fred?"

"What can I do, Bern? I can't leave a baby with Emma. She hasn't got a clue. She would probably leave it on its own in a cot with a ham sandwich and go off climbing all day."

"That's a bit harsh, Fred. Her maternal instinct will kick in."

"I don't think so, not enough anyway. She is really focussed on one thing alone and that is pleasing herself. That's how this happened."

"It pleased you too for a while."

Fred groaned and put his head in his hands.

"I know. Can you imagine what it was like being what she wanted to satisfy her desires? No don't! Let me tell you, ultimately it's scary and not worth it."

"Come on…"

"I know, I know, but I had decided to tell her it was all over. Fresh start etc. I had decided that I would do whatever I could to get Margot and the kids back. But when I got back, she greeted me with this… I'll just have to see it out. You know I need to make sure she doesn't just up and off with my baby. It's not what I wanted, but it's still my baby."

"What a mess. Sophie got the impression that Margot was really sad that you had left so suddenly. Especially for the kids."

Fred rubbed his forehead. "What can I do? Nothing."

"Tell me about Theo and Lucie…" Bernie knew when a subject was done with.

Theo had stayed with Uncle J. The idea of going back to his horrible school in France had been too much to contemplate. Margot could see he was determined and she felt there was nothing to be gained by forcing him to come home.

She'd seen too many teenage disasters not to realise that Theo had been on the brink before. He was so fit and happy now. He was so grateful that his parents agreed to his request that they couldn't help but think it was the right choice. He had suggested himself that he continue his French Bac via distance learning and he was going to work for Jaime creating a better on-line presence and booking systems for the surf school. That way he could train for kite-surfing and pay his way at Uncle J's. Julian was over the moon. As was Lotta, who had been at the local school for the last three years since her mum had moved to Spain permanently.

"It's not the same off season you know." Lotta warned Theo.

"I so do not care about that, I just need to be here." He kissed her and rolled her onto her back. "We may only be sixteen, but we know what we want, don't we?"

She smiled, loving him and kissed him back.

Lucie had been surprised when her dad didn't come straight back. He had promised and she was pretty sure he had decided he wanted Mum back. But then a few days later, good old Snapchat delivered its gut-wrenching news. The Slut was going to have a baby. Typical, the classic trap. Dishonest, manipulating. Lucie hated her, but even when they got home, she wasn't sure she would be able to bring herself to fish out her old Barbie. The baby was her dad's after all, her own brother or sister. She could understand that her dad couldn't abandon it. But she never wanted to lose contact with him again. He treated her like an adult now and he had texted her to promise that they could walk Rufus together every weekend. It was the only thing that made it possible not to see Manté for six weeks. Margot had promised Lucie that they would return to Spain every chance they got. She wanted to as much as Lucie did and she wasn't asking herself why.

Fred had been shocked and ashamed for several days. He hadn't been able to bring himself to ring Margot or the kids and explain. Yet again he had been naive and stupid and yet again there were fundamental consequences. He couldn't believe that he had thought Emma would just give up on an idea so easily. It should have been obvious that she wouldn't let a little matter of morality get in her way. Eventually he pulled himself together enough to pick up the phone to Margot and explain. She had been calm, obviously she knew about the baby already so the first shock had passed. And she knew him and how he functioned. Of course she hadn't known of his plan to win her back...

They discussed Theo's future and found themselves to be on the same wave length as usual. He had seen parents forcing their children down totally unsuitable paths too often. He knew how long a few months were for a teenager and he also knew that you could fall properly in love very young. He hadn't spoken to Lucie or Theo, but he had arranged to come over the first Saturday when they got back. He wrote a long e-mail to Theo and sent the proud photos he had taken of him kite-surfing in the competition. He had told him how great he thought he was and how stupid he had been himself. He decided to let his son digest the e-mail for a while before picking up the phone to him. He was glad that Lotta and Uncle J were there for him.

Emma was bound up in herself as usual and finding work and pregnancy surprisingly tiring. She was asleep so early that she hardly noticed that Fred was going to bed after her and getting up early every morning. They had sex, but she wasn't feeling much like it to be honest. Fred was trying hard to keep things normal, he certainly didn't want her leaving him before the baby was born. He wasn't sure how much claim he would have over the baby if that happened. He had felt the same instant connection to his child when Margot found out she was pregnant with Theo and Lucie. He knew some men had to see the first scan, or even hold the new born baby before they realised they had created a new soul, but not him. He found himself finding excuses to speak to Margot more and more often, there was a lot to be discussed after all with regards to Theo. And anyway, there was no way he was going to lose that connection again. When he had told Emma about Theo's new life, her reaction had been that it was about time he stood on his own two feet. That had really rankled, Theo was only sixteen after all, and his messy life hadn't been his fault.

Fred knew he wasn't really being fair to either Margot or Emma, but then he didn't feel like he had been dealt a fair hand either. He knew he was to blame really, but he just couldn't bring himself to give up on his dream of reuniting his family. It felt like Emma and he were just colleagues who had been taken over by hot sex. Actually, when he thought about it, that is all they ever had been and now they were just colleagues and room-mates who had occasional perfunctory sex.

Margot had been shocked to her core when she first heard the news about Emma's pregnancy. Lucie had put her arm round her mum's waist and shown her an Instagram feed which made it clear. At least it explained why Fred had run away from Spain. She understood him and she knew he couldn't abandon a baby. His sense of protectiveness was part of him. She didn't know how she felt, they were separated anyway. She didn't know if she wanted him back, but it did make things seem very final. She had managed to put a happy slant on things for Lucie and the idea of a baby brother or sister had quite seduced her. She hoped, wryly, that Theo would take note and not rush into things with Lotta. She picked up the phone,

"Hi Jan, we're back, do you fancy coming over for a drink soon?"

"I was just going to phone you! Definitely… Are the rumours which reached me true?"

"I'm afraid so, can you believe it?" It seemed so farcical that she could only laugh about it.

"So Margot, tell me how you are getting on with your young surf dude."

"I e-mailed you about Theo staying in Spain with the love of his life, didn't I?"

"I'm not talking about your Theo, as well you know, I'm talking about your young sexy Spaniard!"

"Hey! He's not that young!"

"Hmph! But he is a dude and a surfer and Spanish?"

"Well yes, but he's not mine."

"Not yet, when are you going back?"

"It's five weeks now. Lucie can't wait and I'll be glad to check in on Theo and Uncle J."

"And…"

"Oh, shut up, you old tart!" Margot laughed, Jan was wicked, but just what she needed.

"Got to live vicariously at my age, my love, and if Fred is about to re-learn the joys of babies, you have no reason not to have some different joys yourself."

"You know, you may be right. I didn't want to be a bad example for the kids, but Theo is on his own little happy cloud and Lucie is a romantic soul."

"There you go…"

"But he's too sweet and I don't want to get involved and it's all too messy."

"That's what you told me before, but I can feel a 'but' now."

Margot just sighed. It was obvious that there was no point in making plans or taking decisions, life just kept pulling the rug from under her feet at the moment.

Chapter Twenty

Emma had been taken aback by Fred when he returned. He looked hotter than in her memory, fit, rested and tanned and somehow less attainable, always an attraction. He'd been surprised by her news, but quite unreadable. He had seemed to get it more quickly than she had. He knew the ropes of course. To celebrate she had sourced a brilliant, high spec baby carrier for him to carry the baby up the mountain with him. Actually, she felt it was quite a bonus that Fred knew about being a dad. She would be able to leave a lot of the nitty-gritty to him, since he would undoubtedly be better at it than her. She would take maternity leave from Christmas since the baby was due in February. If it was a good season she would be skiing by March and properly fit for ski touring in May. Then she would have the easy summer term back at work and be ready to head out to the Andes again with the girls in July. She would be back on top form by then. She was surprised by how tired she was though and quite relieved that Fred was letting her sleep more.

September and October slipped by in the normal busy flurry. Fred got into a routine of seeing Lucie and Rufus for a walk on Saturday mornings. After a week or so it felt natural to have lunch there too. Emma didn't seem to mind that he wasn't at home until mid-afternoon. At one of the Saturday lunchtimes, Fred decided that he had to see Theo sooner rather than later. The only possible time was half term obviously and, equally obviously, it made sense to drive down with Margot and Lucie.

"What do you think, Margot?"

"Fine by me, we're staying for two weeks though."

"I'll get a train back, I only have a week off anyway. I'll only stay for a few days." There were so many things unsaid, but it was OK and Lucie was beaming.

"Brilliant Dad, that is such good news. You hardly saw Manté at all last time."

Margot and Fred smiled at each other, loving their still little girl.

"Emma, I'm going to see Theo at half term."

"What about me?"

"What do you mean, what about you?"

"Well, what am I going to do?"

"I've no idea, whatever you want as usual." Fred was surprised by her question, he really didn't think she'd care. After all, she had simply announced she was leaving for South America for nearly half a year.

"How long are you going for?"

"Just a few days, I haven't booked yet."

"Maybe I'll go and stay with Linda then, a couple of girls nights out would be cool."

Fred nodded, biting back a sigh. He was fairly sure he could trust her not to drink or smoke.

"Sounds like a plan."

Fred was learning very quickly where his priorities lay. He texted Margot to ask her to organise Rafa's studio for him. Then he e-mailed Theo asking him to organise a couple of kite-surf lessons as well. Theo replied instantly, brimming with enthusiasm, to say he'd love to show his dad the ropes and that he was really looking forward to it. Fred's heart swelled.

That evening Emma felt the baby move for the first time.

"Ooh, what was that?"

"What?"

She held her bump with one hand and stroked it with the other.

"Wow!"

"The baby?"

"Quick! Put your hand here."

Fred did, but couldn't feel anything. He put his face to Emma's bump and sang a rumbling version of 'Be my baby' which had always worked marvellously for Theo, although not so much for Lucie. Emma looked at him as though he were mad, but then she felt the baby move again.

"Surreal!"

Fred smiled at her and stroked her tummy. She really had no idea what was in store for her. This little lad, or maybe lass, really needed his daddy.

Margot had made sure that there were no false hopes to be raised at the sight of Fred getting out of the car with them. Or dashed for that matter. She made a point of ringing Theo when she knew he would be at the surf club. She wanted Jaime to know what the real situation was. To be fair she would have been happy to be sure herself. She couldn't decide if she was happy to be driving down to Spain with Fred or not. Obviously, the kids would be happy and that meant a lot. But the hurt was still there, you couldn't forgive that easily. On the other hand, she had loved him before and he hadn't changed, so fundamentally she must still love him. As usual she was an emotional mess. She could only cope by shutting down her feelings and staying practical. From that point of view, sharing the drive could only be a good thing.

Emma hadn't really thought through the idea of a girl's night out. She couldn't drink or have a joint and it wouldn't be easy to dance or flirt with a belly the size of hers. It was still good to see Linda though, she could be so outrageous and at least she got Emma's plans for the future and didn't see any glaring obstacles to them. They found some fun things to do, an escape room, a super chic, gastro-tasting cafe, they got funky nails and had a mud treatment which was apparently just the thing for pregnant women. The baby had liked it too, kicking so hard that the mud cracked. Linda went shopping with her for maternity clothes and they found some pretty cool things. It was better now the bump was obvious, she didn't look simply out-of-shape any longer.

The glow of her break stayed with her afterwards and she was looking forward to Fred getting back. He hadn't asked her to pick him up or anything, he must have left his car near the station. She hadn't asked.

"It's not bad being pregnant actually." Emma was on the phone to her mum. She had felt the urge to speak to her more often than usual in the last few weeks. Her mum had been happy to hear about the baby, but she had a couple of things to say about the fact that Fred was still married and that she hadn't even met him yet. But a grandchild would be welcome, come what may, on an occasional basis anyway.

"Glad to hear it, my girl. You wait until you can only waddle."

"It's not like that any more, Mum. I won't put on too much weight. I'm going to be skiing again by March. The good bit is how you can get anybody to do anything for you, just because!"

"Just because you're worth it I suppose. So what's new,

Emma? You've always wrapped men round your little finger!" Her mum had no illusions about her daughter. "Is he going to get a divorce then?"

"I don't know, haven't thought about it. Does it matter?"

"You have to start thinking about the baby now. Can you afford to do it on your own?"

"How much can it cost? Anyway, stop fretting. Fred's with me now. He sings to the baby you know!"

Emma's mum recognised the signs that her nagging had started having a negative effect. It didn't feel like the teenage years were that far back. So she decided to stop worrying. She had decided a few years ago that if her children were old enough to get into trouble, then they were old enough to get out of it on their own. She couldn't live their lives for them so there was absolutely no point in getting more grey hairs than necessary.

"Have you thought about names yet?"

"No, I fancy something original though." Emma's mum's heart sank at what that might mean.

"Will it take his name?"

"No idea, those things really don't matter do they? They are just bureaucracy."

Her mum said nothing and leant forward for a piece of cake.

Chapter Twenty-one

In the end Fred spent six full days in St Pere. It was long enough for them to generate a sense of normality. He was supposed to go home on Friday morning, but he decided to get the night train back. He'd felt Margot getting used to him being around, they were joking and laughing, working easily domestically. He could still feel the occasional shudder of revulsion when she remembered what he had done, but most of the time it was like old times. Except for the obvious lack of touching of course, but even that was getting less definite. A couple of times, they had, quite naturally, put a hand on a shoulder or thigh. Once they had been squished up together by circumstances on the battered old sofa and they had simply relaxed into it.

As he left, he kissed her gently on the lips. A kiss on the cheek would have been wrong. And their lips had definitely hummed, but he knew she hadn't forgiven him yet. How could she? He was on his way back to another woman's bed, a woman who was having his child. He was kidding himself if he thought there was going to be some kind of happy ending. It was a long train journey and try as he might, he couldn't stop his brain churning the situation relentlessly round and round. By the time the train was trundling along the lake side, he had exhausted his emotional reserves. No more thinking.

When Fred left St Pere a day later than planned, Margot heaved a sigh of relief. It had been nice, but confusing and the moments of anger and emotion had been draining. As she turned away from waving him off, she caught Jaime looking at her quizzically.

"Do you fancy a beer in town, Margot?"

"You know what, Jaime? I really, really do!" It was so typical of Jaime, thoughtful, understanding and simply a good friend. If only he wasn't so damn hot!

The next week flew by, it was beautiful weather, a real Indian summer and they could kite-surf, ride, cycle, eat, drink and be carefree. Margot had been to see Lotta's mum to check that she thought that everything was going well with their kids and had invited her over to eat with them. They really hit it off and Margot had been relieved that there was another adult she could trust to look out for Theo. It also helped dilute the situation with Jaime.

"Let me know if you have any worries, or Theo isn't answering his phone or something, I'm always here."

"Thank you, Caro, that is so good to know. I know he seems to be happy and together now, but last year he really wasn't in a good place."

"OK, well, for what it's worth I think you have done a really brave thing leaving him here and that it is exactly right for him now. You've shown you trust him and that is a big thing." Caro was quiet, but perceptive. Margot hugged her.

"Maybe you could all come to us for Christmas, see the snow and maybe do some skiing? We have room, Lucie can sleep with me, so you can have her room and there is a spare room for Uncle J. We can decide later where Lotta sleeps!" They chuckled, on the same wave length.

"That sounds great. Real snow for Christmas, that would be a first for me. What do you think Julian, would you trust my driving?"

"Sounds great! A log fire, Margot's cooking, what's not to love? Do you know what? I feel a fiesta coming on. Plans and new friends need celebrating. Tomorrow night, to finish off your holiday!"

Uncle J's fiestas were flamboyant affairs. Anyone and everyone were welcome as long as they contributed, be it by wine, song or good humour. And now that his house was looking even more inviting, it was going to be a good one. Rafa was a dab hand with the spit which hung over a big fire pit at the end of the garden. They had an excellent rapport with the local butcher who would provide a pig and throw in some chickens in return for an invite. The bodega would lend a pump for barrels of beer and provide local rosé by the litre on sale or return. The vegetables braised themselves in a tray under the spit and Julian knew from experience that there would be plenty of chorizo, tapas and cakes coming with the guests. A quick phone call and the music was sorted, his masseur had his own band. They played popular covers and a bit of flamenco, perfect for a party!

Margot, Theo and Lucie had yet to experience one of Uncle J's parties. It had been a while since he had felt the impetus, but they were excited and frankly quite amazed by the abrupt change of pace. Lucie suddenly decided she needed a dress and dragged her mum off to the shops. They found her a lovely bright surf dress, perfect with trainers and long teenage legs. Margot found a long skirt and a ruffled top which made her feel gypsy-like and young. Next to the cash desk, they spotted some sparkly bangles they just couldn't resist. Lucie linked her arm through her mum's as they made their way back, admiring the matching bracelets.

"Thanks Mum, that was great and now I'm really looking forward to tonight!" Margot squeezed her arm as a feeling of well-being and optimism flooded through her.

The party started immediately, there was no warm-up, just bang, the sun set and there was a sudden full-on fiesta. The music was fun and easy to dance to, the fire glowed and the smell of roasting pork was tantalising. Drink, conversation and company flowed easily. The fairy-lights, fire-light and topped up summer tans, made everyone look their very best. As the night wore on Margot's inhibitions wore off. She loved dancing in her new swishy skirt. Lucie had some friends from the riding school there, Theo and Lotta were obviously happy and surrounded by mates. Julian was in fine fettle, loving the company. Margot danced with Caro, boys from the club and Jaime, and didn't feel the need to worry about anyone. And then it seemed like she was only dancing with Jaime. He led her by the hand to the other side of the light on the darkened beach and kissed her.

"It's just a kiss, Margot." He whispered in her ear as he stroked her hair, "Come home with me, let's finish this beautiful evening the way we want to." And she did and it was surprisingly lovely.

The next morning Margot was back in her own bed. She had crept out of Jaime's place without waking him up, she hoped. It had been lovely, but that was all. She was pretty sure that it hadn't changed anything between them. She slept late, but then so did everybody. Eventually Rufus started wandering around pushing his face into the comatose bodies who were either in bed or spread wherever, and life started re-surfacing.

Some heads were obviously slightly worse for wear, but the general mood was up-beat. It had been a fitting end of season celebration. The coffee and left-over cake revived them all and the cleaning up was done in no time.

"That was amazing, Uncle J. It just worked, start to finish, no fuss, just fun. You should make a YouTube video, how to host the perfect party." Lucie was impressed.

"At the risk of sounding like a soppy old geezer, all you need is friends, Lucie!"

"I second Lucie, it was really great. You really killed it." Theo stood up and hugged his hospitable uncle. "My social status here is solid now!"

Julian just shrugged and raised an eyebrow. "There's life in the old dog yet, you know!"

And nobody looked at Margot askance at all. Maybe Jaime had been right, it was just a kiss and what happens at fiesta stays at fiesta perhaps? She mentally shook her head, drank her coffee and felt at peace with the world and her happy family.

The second half of term went quickly too. Emma was getting bigger, but she was feeling fine. She couldn't climb, but since her accidents with her shoulder and her hand, it had been quite painful anyway, so she didn't mind too much. It meant she didn't see much of Fred though. At the weekends he was with Lucie or out running up and down mountains with Bernie. They were training for the Pierra Menta and getting quite serious about it. She was still cycling and had started pre-natal yoga. Amongst the friendly bunch of women, there was always one or two who fancied a hike accompanying a qualified mountain leader at the weekend. Every so often she went to stay with Mikela or Linda, even Chloe had found the time to join them once or twice.

As the days got shorter, her evenings got shorter too. She

was usually actually asleep by nine thirty. School started at eight so they were up before seven. Fred had kindly taken on one of her after-school fitness classes, as well as doing his own. He was at the gym twice a week with Bernie as well. That left only Thursday night free, but that was the day they were out on the hill and she was finding it really draining. She was practically asleep before they had eaten.

Fred could see what was happening. He'd seen before what an over-busy timetable could do to a relationship, but this time he really didn't care. The half term week had made him fall completely back in love with Margot, not that he had ever stopped loving her. He had been distracted, led astray, stupid. In the past, stories of men being trapped in ridiculous sordid situations had always made him snort smugly and yet he had let it happen to himself. He thought back to the moment when he had crossed the line with Emma and if he was honest, it was way before that wretched beach party. He had had no right to be staring or smiling or blithely laying his hands on her in an exercise class. He should have known better. Sometime soon, he hoped, he would be able to explain all that to Theo.

"What are we doing for Christmas, Emma?"

"What do you mean?"

"Well, are you thinking of seeing your parents or anything?" Fred had already seen last year how little Christmas meant to Emma, but he thought that maybe the imminent arrival of a baby, might change that. Margot had always loved Christmas, they had a mainly British celebration in their house, excessive, but relaxed and Fred had loved it too. French traditions were equally excessive but very formal. However, Emma neither cooked nor cared about food, so for her, Christmas was neither here nor there.

"I don't think so, they haven't mentioned anything. I suppose we could eat at the Auberge."

Fred sighed inwardly, a meal in a restaurant did not constitute Christmas in his mind. He loved all the little quirks and traditions they had built up over the years as a family. He just wanted to spend the day with them, the kids, Margot, Rufus, his mother-in-law and have a glass of wine too many in front of the fire to finish the day. Instead, they would go to a posh restaurant, eat clinically nice food, and come home to their soulless little apartment to exchange one shop-wrapped gift each.

"Would you like to go to my parents?"

"Oh, I don't think so, it's a long way for one meal." Fred had been thinking of staying, but he was hesitant. His parents had been polite to Emma the one time they had met, but he knew they wouldn't really relish her staying with them. They loved Margot like a daughter and were very unhappy about the irregularity of the whole situation. He didn't really fancy the idea himself if he was honest.

"Actually, I might see what the girls are doing, Mikela will be off on the 25th, her restaurant is always closed. They might like to all get together for a ski."

"You'll have to take it easy by then."

"I know, but Chloe isn't very good anyway, so it's ideal." Emma turned to boil the kettle for a cup of herbal tea. Fred was shunted out again, he picked up his phone to text Margot.

'What are your plans for Christmas? What is Theo doing?'

She replied instantly,

'Didn't I tell you? Theo, Lotta, Caro her mum and Uncle J are all coming here for a few days! It'll be fun. Obviously, Mum will be here too.'

'Can I come too?'

Fred had typed and sent before he could stop himself. The reply did not come back so quickly.

'I don't know, can you?'

'Yes please!'

'Well, the more the merrier… within reason'

Fred thrust his phone up in victory, quickly disguising the movement as a cough. He could spend the day with his family after all.

"You know, it's not a bad idea. It might be the last time you can have a whole day on the slopes for a while."

"You can come too you know."

"With you lot? You must be joking. Listen, we can all have a nice meal on the 24th and I'll pop over and see the kids to give them their presents on the 25th."

The whole thing worked out even better than Fred anticipated. The girls were keen to ski on the 25th, but they all had commitments on the 24th, so they decided to drive through in the morning. Fred suggested that he could sleep on the sofa at Margot's so that there would be room for the girls to stay the night with Emma in the apartment and ski again the next day. In the end, in exchange for driving his mother-in-law home at the end of the day, he got to have a glass or so of wine in front of his own fire with his own dog sleeping at his feet and his family within metres of him. A night of limited comfort on the sofa was a very small price to pay.

The next morning Caro and Margot were sitting drinking a second cup of coffee after breakfast. Fred and Lucie were out for a walk and the other three had yet to surface. "It was a lovely day yesterday, Margot. Thank you so much."

"It was a pleasure. I had a really nice time too."

"I can't believe how civilised you are with Fred. How do you do it?"

"I'm not sure if I'm honest, but I understand him as well as I understand myself and I know how sorry he is and how much he regrets the situation. It still makes me mad as hell sometimes, though."

"I can imagine. Do you think you'll get back together?"

"It doesn't seem as simple as that. There's the baby to consider."

"What? Which baby?"

"His girlfriend is having a baby in a couple of months, February I think."

"Oh my god, what was he doing here yesterday then?"

"It's complicated, I'm not sure myself. I get the feeling she is pretty egotistical and doesn't have a very strong sense of family."

"Well, she is in for a shock in two months' time then!"

"I know!"

"Can I ask you about Jaime? Are you together?"

"No! Where did you get that idea?"

"Well, I was watching you both pretty closely at the party…"

Margot blushed, "I'll be honest with you, we did get together that night, but we are just friends, I don't think anybody else knows. I don't have much experience in these matters, but all I know is that I can't imagine being in a proper relationship with anyone else but Fred. I thought we were for good. On the other hand, I would never have thought I would do what I did that night either."

"You still love Fred then? Would you take him back?" Caro knew she was over-stepping the line, but they had become very good friends very quickly and she needed to know.

"I don't know, I've been trying to avoid the question, but with this baby coming it seems redundant anyway. I have to just live from day to day and see how things turn out. I've realised that you just never know. Who could have foreseen us all being here yesterday altogether?"

And with the sound of steps on the stairs and the back door opening, the time for confidences was over.

Chapter Twenty-two

The baby had arrived a little early. It took an average amount of time and pain to make its appearance, even if for Emma it seemed anything but. She lay spent with one hand on the edge of the cot next to the bed. The sheer lack of control over her body during the birth had been shocking. She had done what she could to breathe through the contractions and push when she was told, but it had been overwhelmingly worse than she had imagined. And she was still having contractions, nobody had warned her that they continued afterwards. The baby was snuffling. She felt totally battered, bruised and helpless. Nobody had brought her anything to eat or drink yet, maybe because it was the middle of the night. She couldn't sleep even though she was exhausted, she just felt like crying.

The morning light made things a bit better. She still had all the pain and mess to cope with and people trying to stuff her nipples into the baby's mouth. The baby didn't fancy it and neither did she. What was wrong with bottles? When Fred arrived just after lunch, he leant over to kiss the baby first and then sat down and put his arms around her. She burst into tears.

"What's the matter? It'll be fine, don't worry." Fred was running out of platitudes as the snot and tears were soaking through his t-shirt. He was worried, the nurses had told him before he came in that Emma was struggling to feed the baby. He hadn't expected that, with Margot it had all come very naturally to her and the first days spent with their tiny babies had been bliss. Emma, on the other hand, seemed to be all over the place.

Then the baby woke up and started yelling. Fred picked him up and had a sniff. His nose told him what to do. It had been a while, but you don't forget how to change a nappy. The baby stopped crying when he heard his daddy's familiar rumbling song and kicked his overly long legs with pleasure. Fred examined his toes, stroked his thighs and rubbed his tummy. Emma watched with amazement. She realised she had never seen a naked new born baby before. He wasn't even the colour she expected and neither was his poo. Suddenly an arc of clear liquid flew up in the air, Fred just laughed and wiped it up. Emma stepped back, horrified.

"Come here little baby, let's get you to your mummy." Fred put the clean baby gently into Emma's unyielding arms. He instantly started rooting for her breast which made her feel quite queasy. Fred sat down next to her with his arm round her shoulders and gently nudged the baby into the right place. And maybe because it was Fred touching her breast and not some unknown bossy uniformed bully, Emma leant back into him, and let the baby take hold. After the initial shock it wasn't so bad.

"I'm not doing this for long, I can tell you."

"That's fine, even three weeks will make all the difference to the baby though."

"That sounds too long to me."

"Ma... let's just see how goes." Fred had been about to say that Margot had breastfed for nine months each time, but he could see that would be a mistake.

"Have you thought about a name?"

"What about Noah?"

"Hey, I like that, I'll go and register him tomorrow morning. Try the other side now."

"Do I have to? He's nearly asleep."

"Come on."

The tears and reluctant feeding continued even after the baby came home. Fred couldn't help thinking that if it had been a first baby for him too, things would be getting tricky. Emma's mother had visited and held the baby stiffly for a couple of minutes before putting him firmly back in his cot. Noah was so surprised that he just lay there looking at her with round eyes.

"You see, no need to molly coddle, babies need some discipline."

Emma did not have the energy to argue and Fred decided he had better put the kettle on.

Mikela and Linda came together and there was plenty of Aunty this and Aunty that, but not a great deal of interaction with Noah. Mikela had been keen, but Noah had started to cry as soon as she held him and that had been enough to put her off. After two and a half weeks of struggling, Fred went to the shops and came back with formula milk and bottles and Noah took to them with pleasure verging on greed.

"I told you I didn't have enough milk. I'm not cut out for this lark."

"Here you hold him, sit there and give him his bottle. He still wants to be with you."

"It's fine, you do this one, he looks happy with you."

And so it went on, Fred knew he needed to get some help for Emma, but she was resisting. He hoped that it would be obvious at the six-week visit, that there was something wrong. The good thing about the bottle was that he would be able to take Noah to meet Lucie and Margot. Maybe it would be a little weird for Margot, but Lucie was desperate to see him.

He turned up as usual for their Saturday morning walk, but with a baby. Nobody can resist a baby and Margot definitely couldn't.

"Hello, Noah." She looked him in the eyes, "Look Lucie, he looks like you!"

Lucie was enraptured, "He's so cute. Look he's got my finger…"

Fred melted at the sight, he hugged them all. Margot just shook her head at him.

"How is Emma? She didn't mind you bringing Noah here?"

Fred just pulled a face. "She was looking forward to some time to herself, she's finding it all quite difficult. She's had to give up feeding him, but it has made it easier for me to take over, obviously."

"She's stopped feeding him, Dad? He must be starving."

"No Lucie, I mean, he's only having bottles now. In fact, he needs one soon, would you like to give it to him?" Lucie blushed when she realised what he meant.

"Oh yes please, I'll just go and wash my hands."

"Good girl." Fred winked at Margot.

"Unbelievable, Fred!"

"I know Margot, but what can I do, it's you who are unbelievable, being so gracious."

Margot dropped a little curtsey, but she was touched in spite of herself.

Lucie sat well tucked into the corner of the settee and Fred put the baby in her arms. She held him perfectly, gently, but firmly and looked him in the eyes. He looked with wonder at her and put his pudgy hand up to grab her hair. Margot leant over to push her hair behind her ears for her, as Fred handed her the bottle.

"Just touch his lips with it, he'll know what to do." Margot realised she had no need to tell Lucie how to give Noah his bottle, she looked like she'd been doing it all her life.

"He's so sweet, so clever, aren't you little baby?" Lucie was in love and Noah spluttered and pulled his mouth away to give her another blue-eyed look of surprise and then settled back into the business at hand. Lucie's heart melted even more.

Margot had had to pinch herself when she first saw Noah. He really looked so much like Lucie had, so much like Fred really, and now she was watching the obvious bonding between brother and sister. She looked over at Fred who was watching the scene with a big soppy grin on his face. He felt her looking and smiled at her with gratitude.

"I need some photos to send Theo."

"Yes Dad, take lots, he's going to love him too."

"Love you, Lucie Loo."

Emma had a strong desire to get back in control. She had a plan before and she saw no reason to change it. So now that she had finally been allowed to stop faffing about with a fretting baby and sore nipples, she could think about getting fit again. She had already lost some of the extra kilos and had started some stretches, but it was time to ramp it up if she was going to be good for skiing. Typically, the snow had been great in January and she had missed it all, but the temperatures had gone up and now it was raining. She was determined though; she had her diet under control and Fred would look after the baby while she went out running. Whenever Noah finally got to sleep in the afternoon, Emma would plug in her earphones and start an Insanity work-out. She would do it without the warm-up as there wasn't time, and with only half of the cool down as she had to get the sweat washed off in time. It was extremely satisfying, she dropped the extra weight in a week, her breasts had gone back to normal and her core was starting to feel more solid.

She started running a bit further, Fred didn't seem to mind, he was better with the baby than she was anyway. It was the end of the runs which were hard, not physically but emotionally. She would start out optimistic and feeling good, but on the home stretch, every time her heel hit the ground, the question 'What have I done?' echoed through her body. She was anxious to get back and check that Noah was OK, but on the other hand she longed for the days when she hadn't had that worry. The rain was depressing too, and their flat smelt strange when she opened the door, it was a mixture of baby and damp washing. The amount of washing to be done amazed her. Noah was only tiny, how come the machine was always full? She loved holding her clean, dry baby, but when he started to wriggle and whine, a sure sign that a full-blown crying session was coming on, she had just one desire and that was to hand him over. She could see that Fred had one desire too, and that was to take Noah in his arms to calm him. She swithered between being relieved and feeling guilty. On the other hand, he was good at it and she was useless, but again, guilty.

"How are you doing Emma? How is little NoNo?" Mikela was ringing on her day off.

"Oh, don't call him that, it sounds awful."

"You should have thought of that before, girlfriend! How are you both?"

"Not too bad, I ran ten K yesterday and I'm finally back down to pre-baby weight."

"Finally? How old is Noah? Five weeks? You're not supposed to do anything but sleep for the first weeks are you? Ten K?"

"It's fine, I hold my bits in when I run. I couldn't stay all blubbery like that any longer."

"And Noah? And your lovely Fred?" Mikela thought Emma had really struck gold with Fred, apart from the glaring fact that he was married to someone else.

"Fred is so good with Noah, he knows what to do. He seems to understand what he needs when he's crying, I have no idea. It just makes me want to run away."

Mikela had a rush of worry, "Just run away for a run, right?"

"Yes, don't panic, it's fine. If I can't cope, I just give him to Fred."

"OooKaay, have you seen a doctor for a check-up yet?"

"Next week, I told you, don't worry."

"Make sure you tell the doctor how you feel. Is it a man or a woman?"

"A woman of course, I don't want a man seeing the mess that it is down there at the moment."

"Emma!"

"Well, it's awful, but it's getting better with the work-outs I'm doing every day."

"You're running ten kilometres and doing a work-out every day? Emma, are you eating properly? What did you have for lunch?"

"Stop fussing, Mikela, it's nothing like that other time, Fred looks after me you know."

Mikela bit her tongue, remembering how she, Linda and Chloe had tried to look after Emma when she became obsessed with exercise and bulimic when they were students. She hoped Emma had told Fred about her troubles in the past, but somehow, she doubted it. Maybe she should tell him herself. Or maybe she would just try and keep watch for the situation getting out of hand. She didn't want him leaving her friend in the lurch, especially with little Noah to consider. She took a deep breath.

"You need to look after yourself Emma, so that you can look after Noah. Sleep when the baby sleeps, you know."

"If I sleep when he sleeps, I can't do my work-out, I told you. You're not listening Mikela. I'm a pro sportswoman, I can do this and I need to do it."

Mikela didn't like the sound of that, but her hands were tied.

Margot had eventually told Jan about what had happened with Jaime. She hadn't told her before, but somehow now she wanted to tell her, having confided in Caro at Christmas. Jan was impressed. She was also surprised that Margot was managing to be so dismissive about it. Somehow, she had imagined a more dramatic result, after all Margot had not had much experience.

"Do you feel a bit more equal with Fred again now?"

"Equal? Hardly, I did it once, he's been at it for a year and half now!"

"Well, I don't suppose he is at the moment, you remember what it's like after a baby."

Margot laughed, "I do, it's amazing there are not more only children!"

"Exactly!"

"If I am completely honest with you, I do feel a little bit of revenge. It's not a very glorious thing to do, but I really wanted to at the time and I also enjoyed it a lot! So there!"

"Go, Margot! Good for you, as you say, why not? Jaime's all right, isn't he?"

"I think so, I think seeing Fred there the week before realigned things for him, he realised that I am not really ready to be a free agent even though I really like him."

"Will you see him again?"

"Of course I'll see him again, but no I don't think we'll sl…"

"Mu-um!" Lucie was calling from the garden, "Come and see what Rufus has found."

Jan and Margot rushed outside. Lucie shushed them and they followed her down to the shed. In front of it, Rufus was lying in a sheltered sunny spot with a kitten asleep on his neck. The kitten's fur was just one shade lighter than Rufus's. Jan snatched her phone from her pocket.

"So cute!"

"Where did it come from?"

"Some cat must have had a litter in the shed. How old do you think it is?"

"Not very, do you think Rufus just let him climb on him or do you think he doesn't know it's there?"

"I don't know Lucie, but I think he must know that it is a baby and so it needs protecting."

"I must send a photo to Theo, Uncle J and Dad. Noah will love it."

Jan glanced at Margot at the mention of Noah. She just shrugged and grinned.

"What can you do? Suddenly we are this modern,

progressive family!" Margot smiled sheepishly at Jan.

Margot and Lucie had not been able to get down to St Pere for much of the holidays, but they had arranged to fly down for three nights over the last weekend. Lucie was anxious to see Manté after so long, worried he would forget her. Margot needed to see Theo, he still needed some face-to-face parenting. Virtual communication was great, but she needed to hold him in her arms and look behind the 2D image, just to check he was doing as well as he seemed to be. The teenage version of checking behind his ears. There was the problem of Rufus though, and his kitten. Margot couldn't really ask Fred to take Rufus, in his small apartment with a new-born baby. She wasn't sure that Emma would be able to cope with the strain. Also, even if the kitten wasn't theirs officially, it seemed to have adopted them and it was too young to leave completely alone. Her mum wouldn't have minded looking after them, but she was away in the UK staying with her sister.

"I'm going to ask your dad to come and look after them Lucie, what do you think?"

"He can come and stay here, with Noah. It'll be nice for Noah to have the garden."

"Do we mind if his mum stays here too?"

"What do you think, Mum? I reckon it's a good thing for Noah to get some fresh air and to get to know Rufus. I mean there's no way you want TS in your bedroom, but she probably won't come anyway."

"TS?"

"Don't ask, Mum." It was another occasion for Margot to just shake her head and not think too hard.

Chapter Twenty-three

Emma's six-week check-up went fine. Her doctor was running late because of a complicated delivery which had run over surgery time and, after all, Emma looked a picture of health. She had lost the baby fat, she was toned and tanned and she didn't have the baby with her which was more efficient. When she was asked about her mood, Emma waxed lyrical about what a supportive father Fred was. Since the doctor knew he had another family and had harboured fears that Emma would find herself on her own with the baby, she was frankly relieved and didn't see the need to push for further information.

"Well, that's fine, you can be intimate again now, as soon as you wish. Everything is back to normal."

Emma was pretty sure that wasn't true, but she wanted to get out. She was missing running time with this stupid appointment.

Fred was worried about Emma, but he was happy looking after Noah himself. They had decided he would have two-thirds of the parental leave available which should work out. At least when he was responsible for the child-care, he knew it was being done properly. The spring holidays came at the end of the leave and Emma was dying to get back out on skis. Fred had been disappointed by the snow the last couple of times he had been out and as it had been raining since, it could only be worse. Anyway, he was sure he would rather take care of his little boy. He knew how quickly kids grew up and he wanted to make the most of every minute possible.

"I tell you what Emma, why don't I take Noah to stay with my mum and dad for a couple of days during the holidays, and you could get your friends over like you did at Christmas. Mum and Dad will be glad to spend some time with Noah."

Emma went through a whirlwind of emotions in reaction to Fred's suggestion, she disliked his parents, but they were quite wealthy and they were Noah's grandparents. She really, really wanted a girl's break skiing, but she didn't want anyone to think she was a bad mother. A complete break from the baby and holier-than-thou Fred would be a relief. She would miss them of course, but she should start as she meant to carry on. Control, that was what she needed, what she craved. She could be in control again if they were somewhere else.

"Yes, what a great idea. Will you be able to manage?" Fred looked at her and raised his eyebrows, but wisely said nothing, just nodded.

Emma was much better after her break with her friends. Her faith had been restored in her future life. She felt it would be possible to continue to be herself and do things she loved doing, whilst having the cute little baby to cuddle. The feeling of well-being lasted for about three days. Fred was working Thursday and Friday and long days at that. Emma had strapped the baby into the baby carrier and set out on a long walk the first day, but Noah didn't seem to like that much. He was fine for the first half hour, but then the tell-tale fidget started. After another half hour of stopping and starting and Noah crying harder and harder, Emma had to admit defeat. That left the whole of the day to get through and the next. By Friday evening she was had resorted to wearing her earphones with music at full blast to ignore the noise. Luckily the only neighbour who didn't work was the old lady next door who was pretty deaf.

When Fred got home, he found Emma doing a flamingo pose, hair swept off her face with a head band, eyes closed and earphones in. He looked round for Noah. He was asleep, fallen forward and half slipping out of his bouncy chair. His tufts of hair were stuck to his forehead and he was flushed and tear stained. It was a frightening sight. Fred gently disentangled him from the straps of the chair and held him close as a mighty sob shuddered through his hot little body. He opened his eyes and started to cry again. Fred blew on his face, breathed in his odour and started talking to the distraught little baby as he made a bee-line for the bathroom. In a couple of efficient moves he had the baby bath filling, the dirty nappy off and Noah wrapped in a towel looking at himself in the mirror. Noah scowled at the face in the mirror, still engulfed in his unhappiness, but then his dad's face popped into view and then disappeared again. There it was again, with a big smile on it. Gone again! Back again! Noah gave a little smile and suddenly he was chuckling, all his cares gone. Fred lowered him into the warm water and splashed some of it over his head. The baby relaxed, enjoying the sensation and then he remembered how to splash. Sure, it was messy, but the result was a happy, clean, sleepy baby who was ready for his bottle and his bed.

Emma redeemed herself to some extent by having a bottle ready, she handed it to Fred silently and he sat down in the chair next to the cot, settling himself in to read Noah a story. Emma couldn't understand why he read a story every night to a baby who obviously couldn't understand it. Most of them had been Theo and Lucie's which meant that many were in English. But it felt as natural as rain to Fred and he would not be put off doing it. Emma left him to it and went to have a quick shower.

"Did you have a bad day?" Fred came through, having got Noah to sleep and spun a cloth around the sopping bathroom.

"He just wouldn't stop crying. I thought it was bad yesterday, but today it was relentless. He just doesn't like being with me."

"It's not that, you have to stop thinking that. You need a kind of mental checklist, does he need changing, food, water, to move, a chat, a cuddle… you know!"

"I can't do it, once the noise starts, all my logic just flies out the window. And everything I offer him seems to make him scream louder."

Fred knew when to stop and when to just offer comfort, but he also knew he was going to have to sort something out.

"A glass of wine will help and I'll make us a tartiflette, someone gave me a Reblochon today. Did you have any lunch?" He suspected that she wasn't eating when he wasn't around, no wonder she was on edge. "Sit down. Here. Cheers."

"Listen, Margot asked me to look after Rufus and his kitten for three nights next weekend. In fact, she said we could all stay there, but I thought that would be too weird."

"Rufus's kitten?"

"Long story! I was thinking I would just go backwards and forwards to see Rufus, even if he doesn't like sleeping on his own."

"He's a dog!"

"I know, but still. But I've just had a better idea, why don't Noah and I go and you go and stay with Linda? Or she can come here again."

Emma did not need talking round. The snow was not good,

it had rained and frozen and she had to admit to a certain unease on skis. She had no desire to hurt herself again, on the other hand a night out in Lyon was a different story. She could have a drink again, she knew she looked good again, there were no dodgy blobby bits left to cover up. The thought of dressing up and going out looking like a real girl was bliss.

"Ooh Fred, that sounds great. I could go on Thursday."

"Who will look after Noah then? No tell you what, I'll take Friday off. I have a lieu day due, then you can drive over on Friday morning."

"Couldn't you try and get home early on Thursday? That way I could drive over for the evening."

"Wow, um OK, I suppose I could try." Fred was shocked, she really couldn't wait to get away from them. He was still hoping Emma's maternal instinct would get stronger, but it didn't seem to be happening. To be fair, he wondered if he was engineering situations to suit his own purposes.

"Look at the picture Lucie sent me of the kitten. She wanted me to show it to Noah."

Emma glanced and shrugged, "Yep, cute." She did not like Lucie. She hadn't seen her to talk to since she and Fred had got together, but she had seen online comments and Fred's look of absolute adoration whenever he talked about her. For the few days after she had given Noah a bottle for the first time, Fred had not been able to help himself. Everybody, right down to the postman, had been shown the photo of Lucie holding the baby. Lucie herself had posted the photo everywhere. The comments had all been sick-making. It wasn't normal for a thirteen-year-old girl to be so saintly and get on so well with both parents. Surely the trauma and separation should have made her kick off, but no she had just become an expert rider… Emma looked back at how she had been at thirteen, she had pushed every boundary she could and had only avoided disaster with expert use of condoms and a terrible fear of needles. It had taken years for her hair to recover from the onslaught of chemicals it had suffered. Still, what the hell, she was going to have a night out on the tiles with her best buds. Who cared about Little Miss Loo?

Chapter Twenty-four

When Margot and Lucie arrived at San Pere, their whole second family was gathered on the terrace. There had been a subtle shift in the dynamics since Christmas. Theo seemed more grown up than ever, caring for his elderly uncle, more than being cared for. He was still very obviously as much in love with Lotta as ever. Caro had become part of the family now too. She and Jaime were bustling around in the kitchen preparing a welcome meal. They were casually at ease with each other. Margot thought back to Caro's questions at Christmas and pushed down a little green stab of jealousy. She didn't think they were together yet and indeed Jaime held her tight and stroked her hair when she arrived, but she didn't think it would be long. It was good really, perfect even. They matched, they both had the same lifestyle and lived in the same place for goodness' sake! Anyway, she had firmly said she wasn't interested, but it still hurt a bit.

"How is my favourite niece? I'm so glad you could come, even if it is for a flying visit." Julian kept hugging her. "I've missed you, guapita."

"I've missed you too, Uncle J. We'll come for longer next time and for weeks in the summer. You'll be sick of us!"

"Never, never, never. Even though I have my Theo and little Lotta, we all need you."

Margot hugged and planted a kiss on his brown cheek, she knew what he was doing. It was amazing how well they read each other, amazing and wonderful.

"What have you done with my favourite loopy pooch?"

"You'll never believe it! Fred is staying with Noah at home to look after Rufus and Marigold."

"Marigold? Who is Marigold?" Theo had a note of panic in his voice.

"Rufus's kitten!"

"You called it Marigold? Like rubber gloves?"

"Shut up, Theo, like the flower, she's orange and gorgeous and Rufus loves her."

"I'm not sure he does Lucie, but it's true he puts up with anything she does. She sleeps on his head, between his paws, tried to swing on his tail, eats his food when he does. It's unbelievable. You've never seen anything like it, Uncle J. Before he chased any cat he saw."

"True love, makes mush out of many a man!" Uncle J clocked his head at Theo, who punched him good-naturedly in his firmly protruding stomach. "And how is little Noah, Lucie?" Uncle J was wise in his questioning.

"Lovely, so cute. You've got to meet him. Especially you Theo. He's your brother!"

Although Theo knew that Margot and Lucie had seen the baby, in typical teenage male fashion, he had not really let it impinge on him. He was taken aback by Lucie's enthusiasm. He glanced at Margot, who was still smiling.

"I hadn't really thought of it like that, but I suppose he is."

"Actually Theo, he looks so like you and Lucie did when you were little, and he didn't ask for anything."

Theo grabbed his mum into an enveloping hug, "You are something else, Mum, it's really good to see you." Both Margot and Uncle J had to wipe their eyes sheepishly.

"Time for a drink I think." Jaime handed round glasses of local rosé. "What shall we drink to? The baby's health? Family reunions?"

"To a good day kite-surfing tomorrow, Jaime!" Margot needed to dampen down the emotions before they were all over-whelmed by them.

"Great! To tomorrow!" They all raised their glasses.

The weekend went too quickly. Lucie had spent as much time as possible with Manté, while Margot kite-surfed with Theo and Jaime. Caro had found time to grab Margot for a quiet word over a coffee in her bar.

"No regrets, Margot?"

Margot understood immediately. "None whatsoever." She smiled and patted Caro's hand. Caro blushed and relaxed, smiling her thanks.

After her initial feeling of 'oy, get off, he's mine', Margot actually felt relief. She didn't have to decide any more, to analyse her feelings or worry about Jaime. The journey home went smoothly, even if it wasn't much quicker than driving door to door. It made a change to fly and it meant she wasn't exhausted from driving, but even so, when they drove into their village Margot heaved a sigh of relief.

"It was a long way for three days, but it was worth it wasn't it, Lucie?"

"Yes Mum, but next time we've got to stay longer. Manté looked so sad when I told him we were leaving already."

"You told him we'd be back though?"

"Of course, but still. Hey look! Dad's still here! Yeh!"

Margot smiled, somehow Lucie's simplistic way of looking at things seemed blindingly right.

"Hey, Fred." Margot got out of the car, pushing down an

eager Rufus who seemed to know where they had been. Fred had a dozing Noah in his arms and she put a hand on his free shoulder and kissed him on both cheeks. Fred responded instinctively, in spite of a slightly surprised look on his face. Margot didn't care, she was going to live life like Lucie, optimistic and in the moment, no rancour, no regrets, a new happy her.

"Here, can you grab Noah a minute, Margot?" Fred stuffed the sleepy baby in her arms quite naturally and grabbed Lucie for a massive whirl-around hug.

"Dad, put me down, I'm too big for that!"

"No way, not yet, Luce." But he did put her down, she was really too tall for it even if she didn't weigh much.

Margot cuddled the baby into her, sniffing his head. The intoxicating smell of baby scalp whisking her back to the days of believing in happy ever after. As Fred, Lucie and Rufus untangled themselves, Lucie was desperate to hold Noah.

"Did you have a nice weekend, Noah? Did you see the stars in my bedroom? Where's Marigold, Dad?"

"Actually, I'm not sure, I saw her a little while ago. She's probably asleep on a chair somewhere."

"Inside?" Margot looked horrified.

"Well yes, isn't she allowed? You didn't say." Which was true, she hadn't, well it was too late now.

"It doesn't really matter." Then she caught Fred winking at Lucie and realised that she'd been set up. "Hey you two are terrible!" She was laughing though, having the kitten in the house was probably inevitable.

"How were Theo and Uncle J, and Manté of course?"

"All great, they all send their love."

"Guess what? Noah slept through two nights in a row. It's

just so calm here."

Margot just nodded, she still needed to perfect the no rancour part of her new creed.

"Well, I better get off, you have to be up early in the morning, don't you? I just wanted to hear the news and check you were home safely."

"Well thanks Fred, it really saved the day for us. I wouldn't have been happy leaving poor old Rufus with just a daily visit."

"No neither would he, I don't think. But all in all, he's a lucky dog. See you next Saturday?"

"Sure."

"Bring Noah, OK, Dad?"

"Of course, he wouldn't miss seeing his big sister."

As Lucie was heading up to bed, she put her head on her mum's shoulder from behind.

"Dad never talks about TS, does he? Theo says Lotta every other word. And Dad seems to be looking after Noah nearly all the time, doesn't he? Do you think she's not keen on being a mum?"

"I don't know Lucie, it does seem a bit strange, but it's none of our business. I do think that you must start calling TS 'Emma' from now on though, for Noah's sake!"

"Mum!" Lucie burst out laughing at hearing her mum say TS. She chuckled all the way up the stairs, life was good.

The good feeling lasted until Friday when Lucie suddenly started feeling really unwell. She ran a temperature at school and had to come home. Her body was aching and her throat was as sore as she had ever known it. Margot picked her up from school and put her to bed with paracetamol and blankets. She was very hot and shivering violently.

"This is a nasty bug Lucie, hopefully you'll sleep it off and feel better in the morning."

Margot didn't need a thermometer to know that this wasn't just tonsillitis. After a bumpy night, Lucie was not better. She was still running a fever and had severe abdominal pains. When Margot helped her to get up to go to the loo, she could hardly stand. In spite of the good weather at the weekend, she was as pale as her hair. She looked wretched. Margot picked up her phone to call Fred, she had no patience for texting in situations like this.

"Fred, it's me. Listen, Lucie is ill, some kind of virus. I think she needs to see a doctor. Don't bring Noah over, in fact you'd better not come, you don't want to take the bug home with you. Lucie is in no fit state anyway."

Fred was shocked, usually Margot was so calm and she was used to illness after all. Lucie must be bad.

"Can you get a doctor to come out over the weekend?"

"I suppose I can ask Françoise to come. I'm sure she wouldn't mind, but I'll just monitor her until Monday, she should be over the worst by then."

"You're the pro Margot, you'll know what to do, trust your instincts."

"Thanks, Fred. Speak soon," And the phone was down. There was no way Fred could leave her to cope on her own, she sounded really worried. Emma could manage Noah by herself for the day. An hour later, he walked into the house, calling softly.

"Fred." Margot arrived at the top of the stairs. "You came."

"Course I came. How is she?"

"She's asleep. I'm scared for some reason. Scared it's serious, she was so happy and healthy and suddenly, bang. Her temperature is extremely high and her glands are really swollen."

"Call your friend, get her over. You'd advise a patient to see a doctor, wouldn't you?"

"You're right." Fred gathered her into his arms and for a minute, she leant into their comfort.

In the end, a conversation with her doctor friend and Fred's reassuring presence meant that Margot felt she could wait until Monday to see how Lucie was. On Monday the friendly G.P. came and examined Lucie and took some blood, advising the traditional ice-cream or sorbet as a cure for the sore throat. Lucie managed a weak smile at that.

"I'll show you out, Françoise, and then I'll dig you out some ice-cream, Lucie."

Out of ear-shot of Lucie, Françoise smiled at the nurse turned anxious mother who was standing in front of her.

"I think we'll find it's glandular fever, Margot, not the leukaemia you are worrying about."

"Thanks, Françoise. I know it's not like me to panic, she just looked so diminished and it's all been a bit emotional recently."

"Well glandular fever can be bad too, but it does get better. The worst bit will be over in about three weeks, no sport for longer though. Her spleen is pretty swollen, if it gets suddenly much more acute, then react. Otherwise, you need to keep her temperature down and give her some TLC. She might feel quite sorry for herself. The test results will be back by Wednesday, but really I'm pretty sure it'll be fine."

Margot nodded, relieved. Glandular fever might drag on, but it was so much better than the alternatives. She waved off her friend and called Fred who picked up instantly. The relief in his voice was palpable.

"Lucky Manté is so far away. We'd have a job keeping her from riding him. I'll be over later with more fancy ice-creams than you've ever seen. Noah can have his nap in the car."

"I can't believe how often I keep saying thanks Fred, but thanks."

Chapter Twenty-five

Emma had a brilliant weekend with Linda. She had relished the sheer girliness of it. She had even found someone to flirt with in one of the many bars they had visited on the Friday night. He was cool, but when he asked for her number, a picture of Noah in Fred's arms swam in front of her eyes, sobering her suddenly. She didn't want to rock the boat. Fred might just walk out on her. Even worse, he might walk out on her and Noah. Single motherhood was not something she wanted to imagine. Once they got past this stage, things would be better. Babies are just so dependant. Once Noah could walk and talk, surely life would be easier. She said as much to her friends, who did a good job of hiding their disbelief.

It was unbelievable really that she had been the one to start all this. She really needed to try and be slightly less impulsive at times, but it wasn't in her. On the Saturday night, they had gone to see a new DJ who was gaining a fierce reputation. The atmosphere was amazing, so different to the sleepy market town where she lived. Linda knew everybody and Emma found herself on her own for a while. Not for long though, a young guy leant into her ear to make conversation. It was impossible, so he took her hand and dragged her off to dance. The music was great and the guy knew how to dance. Eventually though they had to rest, he took her hand and lead her out onto a terrace. There was a fantastic view over old Lyon and the heaters and fairy lights made the place look magical. The guy simply kissed her, no hesitation or conversation, just almost forgotten sensations. Who wrote the rule book anyway? Emma kissed him back, pushing back any remaining thoughts. But then she felt a sharp tap on her shoulder.

"Time to go, Emma?" Linda didn't want to be held responsible by anybody. If Emma really wanted to play things that way, then all hail to her, but she needed to check she was thinking straight first. That conversation could wait till the morning, well, later that morning anyway.

In the end Linda had held off from an inquisition. She didn't really want to get involved, Emma had made her own choices and would continue to do so. She was no innocent young girl who needed protection. Next time she would stay well out of it. Emma was grateful to Linda on all accounts. She had a great weekend, not done anything stupid and hadn't had to dissect her actions or intentions afterwards. It would all be fine.

Unfortunately, the weekend after Lucie had got ill which meant that Emma had to change her plans to go hiking on Saturday. It was frustrating, she'd planned an interesting walk for a couple of the people she knew from the Club Alpin and she didn't like letting them down. It was annoying of Fred to leave her holding the baby.

Over the next fortnight Lucie did get better. She wasn't back at school and was still running the occasional surprisingly high temperature, but the results had come back confirming glandular fever and nothing worse which was the main thing. Fred popped over as often as he could, every day on the days he wasn't working and at the weekends. Margot had to work and Lucie needed the company and looking after. It worked out.

One day, Bernie hailed Emma to see if she knew where Fred was as he wasn't answering his phone.

"Oh, he's probably at Margot's, looking after Lucie as usual." Bernie looked surprised and pleased, before he could disguise his reaction. It made Emma think. Maybe she was being a little complacent. Maybe Margot wanted Fred back after all. She poked around her feelings and couldn't decide what she felt. What was certain was that she didn't want to lose out to an over-weight, middle-aged nurse. She needed to up her game a bit. Maybe they should try a little holiday. Fred's parents, or even her mum would probably look after Noah for a few days. On the other hand, she baulked at the idea of poor little Noah in either of those households. Maybe they should have a family holiday somewhere nice. Sardinia might fit the bill, something romantic and wild, but still child friendly and not too far away.

She spent the next couple of evenings looking for a plan. By Wednesday evening, it was organised, if not yet booked. Over a civilised meal prepared by Fred, she got out her phone.

"So, I have a suggestion. A family holiday in Sardinia during the Easter break. Look, I've found some flights, a rental and a car. What do you think?"

"Well, Lucie is much better, I think they will be able to go down to Spain." Fred saw Emma's downcast expression and finally caught up with her thinking. He took the proffered olive branch, "That sounds great!"

"OK, well click on 'confirm booking' then."

"Maybe I should just check with Ma…" but he saw Emma's face. "Yes, here goes!" And he clicked, after all a family holiday did seem like a good idea.

The next few weeks slipped by. Lucie was improving steadily, but she still appreciated her dad being on hand so readily. She was getting excited about spending two weeks in San Pere and Fred was sure that the change of climate would do her good. He wasn't so sure about her riding so soon. He hoped Margot would sort that out. He was also hoping that a week away would be beneficial for him and Emma too. They really didn't seem to spend much time together, the three of them.

In the end, the fortnight in Spain was the perfect convalescence for Lucie. She didn't feel like riding yet, but she could groom Manté to her heart's content. Margot kite-surfed with Theo. Caro and Jaime were holding hands and Uncle J was trying out even more recipes. He wouldn't let his little Lucie lift a finger, he blended delicious smoothies for her, made sure she had plenty of spinach and sweet local oranges and even read her stories. Lucie discovered that you are never too old to be read to and it was the perfect antidote to the waves of debilitating tiredness which still engulfed her from time to time. Margot was relieved to see Lucie getting back to full health and also to have someone else to share the worry with full time. It was true that Fred had been great, but he always had to scuttle off. She needed more time to talk and simply relax.

The week in Sardinia did not go so smoothly. The car hire had been complicated, blocking one credit card completely and the apartment they had rented was only just clean. This was coupled with an extremely ancient and rickety cot for Noah and then the double bed in the photo turned out to be two singles pushed together with hard iron edges down the middle. Not as romantic as Emma had hoped. The albeit ecological system for disposing of 'wet waste' was complicated and embarrassing. Nothing at all was allowed in the toilet, it was all a bit revealing. Nappies, which are always a nuisance, became nightmarish to get rid of. Hardly any shops or restaurants were open, it was too early in the season. This meant that much advance planning was needed, the opposite to the spontaneous relaxing time she had been hoping for. The evenings were chilly and mosquito ridden, so they spent them on the upright chairs around a Formica table rather than in the romantic, scented garden overlooking the sea. The island was very beautiful, it was covered in spring flowers and the beaches were all pristine. Everywhere there were tempting lanes and tracks to run on, but of course they had to take it in turns while the other babysat. They did have some lovely moments, spectacular sunsets, the first time Noah felt sand (until he put it in his mouth) and the first time a little wave trickled over his toes (until he tasted the salty water) and some intimate snatched moments while Noah slept. These moments seemed to be little bubbles of happiness in a general feeling of hard work, coupled with boredom. It was not the idyllic family bonding experience they had hoped for.

"Do you think it'll get easier, Fred? Everything just seems to be such an effort."

"Course it will, it just takes a bit of getting used to, that's all. By the end of the summer, you'll be a natural, you'll forget you ever found it hard." Privately Fred wasn't so sure, as far as he remembered, the baby stage was the easiest. Kids basically got heavier, more expensive, slept less and answered back more as they got older.

"I'll be in South America this summer, so I doubt it."

"What? South America?"

"Well yes, you know that. We're going to finish our trip. Actually, it's pretty exciting, I forgot to tell you, Linda has found a production company who want to film us. There may be quite a bit of promo work to do too."

Fred thought he'd got used to Emma's way of thinking, but he really hadn't imagined she would try to repeat last summer now that Noah was here.

"What about Noah?"

"Well, you can look after him, can't you?"

"You could've run it by me first. What if I had plans of my own?"

"Well obviously you haven't, you wouldn't leave Noah for three months, would you?"

She amazed him at times. Poor little Noah. Fred looked at her with her bleached, blue tipped pixie cut, he really didn't like either dyed or short hair, at her toned body without an ounce of maternal softness and her unconcerned eyes and asked himself yet again how he had got into this position. He'd been hoodwinked, tantalised by her youth and devil-may-care attitude. Well, that attitude was making itself felt. He sighed inwardly and said nothing, there was nothing to say.

Chapter Twenty-six

May passed in a flash, there were the long weekends, school trips, exams to organise. Fred and Emma started to manage things better, Emma became more adept with Noah. Bernie's Sophie helped out too, managing to give Emma some well-directed advice without putting her back up. And then it was June, and Emma was off. She had a moment of doubt as she leant over Noah's sleeping form on the morning of her departure. He was so cute asleep. He wouldn't remember this though. His dad would take care of him far better than she could herself. There was nothing to worry about or to feel guilty about. Then her phone vibrated, it was Linda, they were ten minutes away. They were picking her up with the camera rolling. Hopefully Fred would play along and kiss her goodbye with feeling. He had agreed to that, but not to Noah being filmed and to be honest she thought he was right. He did play along, kissed her and wished her bon voyage and waved goodbye. He wasn't exactly smiling into the camera, but he was fairly gracious.

"I'll miss you," she whispered. He just gave her a gentle push towards the minibus and waved at the others.

There were two more weeks of school. Fortunately, Lucie had already finished and had agreed to come and stay for the two days a week that Fred had to work. She was really looking forward to looking after Noah. Margot was happy with the solution as it meant Lucie wouldn't be left alone for too long and Fred wouldn't be far away if she needed him.

The first day Fred came home to find Lucie and Noah rolling on the floor giggling with glee. Lucie was ducking behind a cushion in a long game of pee-po and Noah was loving it. Earlier Fred had managed to pop home during his lunch break just to check, and had found Lucie happily sketching and Noah fast asleep in his cot. Now he came back to this happy carefree scene which he couldn't help comparing to his normal home-coming. He lay on the floor with the two of them and joined in, delighting in Noah's infectious giggle.

"Look at this, Dad!" Lucie burbled some baby sounds while smiling at Noah and Noah repeated them, smiling back at her.

"Wow! What a clever boy you are, my little lad. And what a great big sister you have! Did you have any problems, Lucie?"

"Well, he did cry a bit when he woke up, but I changed him and gave him some water and he was fine. Then we went for a walk and then we played. It was fun!"

Fred scooped up Noah and pulled Lucie to her feet. "We are so lucky to have you, Luce. Time for Noah's bath now I think."

"Cool!"

Fred texted Margot from bed that night, knowing she'd be dying to hear how Lucie had got on.

Came back to a blissfully happy scene. Lucie has been fantastic. Noah just loves her!'

Thanks for letting me know Fred. Lunch on Saturday?

Great! We'll be there for Rufus as usual.

OK, see you. x

As Margot pushed the send button, she realised she had added an 'x' without thinking. It was definitely inappropriate, but it was best not to make a big thing about it. There were 'x's galore these days, but then her phone pinged again.

Looking forward to it, night x.

She groaned. That felt wrong, but she had to look on the bright side, she was so proud of her little girl. She had texted Lucie earlier, of course, and she had already known that things had gone well, but Fred's endorsement felt good. She really wanted to share her feelings with someone, she picked up the phone and rang Uncle J.

"Hey, Uncle J!"

"Hey yourself Margot, you just love rhyming, don't you?"

"I do, I do, how are you?"

"Enough!" Julian was chuckling. "I'm fine. What has you ringing me this fine evening?"

"Lucie's at Fred's. She's baby-sitting Noah for two days."

"Where's his mother?"

"South America."

"South America? Doing what?"

"Finishing off her flaming bike ride."

"And leaving little Noah on his own."

"Well, no, with Fred, but yes."

"Good grief! How long for?"

"Three months I think."

"Three months? A mother doesn't leave a little baby for

three months."

"Well, this one has."

"You'd better invite them here for the summer. Lucie and Theo can help with their baby brother and they'll see their dad."

"Uncle J..." Margot's tone was warning.

"Yes, love?"

"No meddling!"

"Would I? Just ask him. He may as well be here than on his own with the little one."

Margot put down the phone pensively, having wished her lovely old uncle a fond good night. He could be right. Lucie was really taken with Noah and Theo needed his dad. What it would be like for her didn't seem to count.

"So Fred, Uncle Julian wondered if you and Noah would like to join us this summer? Unless you have other plans?" Fred's mouth, fell open.

"Really? My god, that would be fantastic. But what about you, Margot? It's a lot to ask." At least somebody was thinking about her feelings, but Lucie jumped in.

"Oh Dad, that's brilliant. Noah will grow up so much in two months, I don't want to miss anything. He might even start crawling, eh, Noah?" Noah banged his plastic keys on the side of his bouncy chair and blew bubbles at his big sister. He was in pride of place on the kitchen table as they ate their usual Saturday lunch.

"Well Fred, I wouldn't have passed the message on if I didn't think I could handle it."

"Wow, just wow. I was wondering if I would go a bit stir crazy in the apartment with just the two of us. Especially not being able to see you all at the weekends." Rufus heard the emotion and stood up from his usual position under the table to put his head on Fred's thigh. "And you Rufus, I would have missed you too. But will there be room?"

"That's something else Julian mentioned the other night. Theo and Lotta are moving in together."

"How can he afford that?"

"Well, it's pretty convenient actually. Jaime is moving in with Caro, so Theo and Lotta can have his place."

Fred shook his head with disbelief.

"It seems like a big step."

"I know, but it's probably better than what usually seems to happen these days. You know, when the girlfriend or boyfriend gradually move in with one set of parents and they continue to act and be treated like kids."

"You're right. That sounds like hell from what I've heard. There's no fun like there was when we used to have to creep about at night."

"Dad!"

"Sorry Luce, sorry Margot. But actually, it sounds very practical and amazingly civilised and there'll be a room for me and Noah!"

"Exactly!"

"Noah loved the sea in Sardinia, until he tasted it, didn't you, Noah?"

"Also, you'll have some willing baby-sitters, so you'll be able to do some things for yourself."

"I don't know about that, but it's true I was wondering how I was going to keep my fitness levels up. But just to have company and especially to be with my family, I can't believe it." Fred looked almost tearful.

"Do you need to run it by Emma?" Margot felt the need to apply some brakes to the situation.

"I don't think so, it's really up to me under the circumstances."

"Cool, the journey will be much easier."

"Maybe you've forgotten what it's like to travel with a little baby!"

"But you are such a good little chap aren't you, Noah?" Margot smiled at Noah who kicked his feet and chuckled in agreement.

Chapter Twenty-seven

Fred had decided to leave it up to Emma when and how she wanted to make contact. It was a test he supposed, to see whether it was a case of absence made the heart grow fonder or out of sight, out of mind. He knew the girls were going to be pressurised into making an 'interesting piece of reality T.V.', so he didn't really want to know all the details. He'd seen enough of the photos on Instagram last time to be able to imagine how it might play out. They were a bunch of good-looking young women after all. He shook his head, wondering how his life had got so messy and why on earth social media seemed to be playing such a big part in it.

Emma was loving every second of the trip. The joy of being able to have a drink on the plane without worrying about it being spilt, of dozing off without being woken up, of having uninterrupted conversations with different people. The joys of being child-free in short. There were not only her friends, but also a crew of three who would be following them. There was a cameraman, a sound guy and a girl who was gopher and driver. They were young and bright and revelling in the adventure of filming in Chile. Karl the cameraman was constantly filming, sometimes just with a phone, but it was pretty much one hundred percent of the time. Emma realised that they would soon become oblivious to it, she wasn't sure how she felt about that.

The morning after their arrival, they had set up their bikes and the crew had located their van. They didn't intend to be in convoy the whole time as it would take away much of the challenge if they had a support vehicle with them at all times. Sometimes the van would go on ahead, sometimes they would hold back. The idea was to catch spontaneous shots when possible and if unavoidable, re-stage specific incidents. The evenings would be spent together, turning it into a 'making of' documentary at the same time.

"How is your shoulder, Linda?" Chloe was doing some intense looking stretches

"Good thanks. One hundred percent."

"And how is your fitness this time, Emma?" Emma bristled, that was not an innocent comment. Julie, the driver, nudged Karl, sensing a nice film-able bit of bitching coming up.

"I'm fine thanks, Chloe. Never better!" She leapt into a deep lunge on one leg and then the other.

Karl focussed on her sharply defined buttocks as she went down again.

"Glad to hear it. Mikela, did you do a little bit of training at least." Mikela just shook her head in mock despair at her uppity friend and smiled.

"It's OK, I'll get fit as I go. I'm looking forward to losing a couple of kilos."

"I can imagine."

Stephen, the sound guy, was leaping around with his microphone, but at this he winked at Mikela and shook his head in disagreement. With her bouncy, curly, chestnut hair and her bouncy, curvy, chocolate brown body, he couldn't imagine she needed to lose anything.

"No way," he muttered under his breath. Mikela looked at

him in surprise.

"Oh god." Chloe hadn't finished. "Well, this year, there's no going slow, no half measures. This time we're getting it done." She pulled her foot up to her buttock, stretching her skinny thigh, emphasising her bony arms. Her cycling had taken a more serious turn recently and she knew that as far as her career was concerned, it was now or never. Very soon it would be too late. She had dropped every last gram of superfluous fat over the last year. She was wearing her pretty blond hair scraped back off her face, in a tight pony tail and she looked like she'd forgotten her smiling skills with the stresses of the competition circuit. Her trainer had thought that some recreational, or at least different cycling, would be good for her mentally, which was why she had made time to come, but she wasn't going to let anything slip, even so.

Linda groaned, and winked at Karl, she had a feel for what would make good footage. She herself had prepared thoroughly for the trip. Her layered haircut was strategically planned to grow out nicely and was already blond. She had had her teeth whitened and was waxed to within an inch of her life. Her new cycling gear was top of the range and subtle. She had toned up in the gym and she knew she was in good shape. Fair enough, it wasn't a competition, but she still wanted to win. She liked teaching well enough, but she wouldn't say no to change in career. Something more glamorous or exotic would be perfect for her thirties.

"So, girls! Are we ready for a group photo? Come here, Emma. Ready? Queso!"

And so, to start their South American adventure, Part Two, Linda was in the middle showing off her new white smile, with her arms round a grinning Emma and Mikela and Chloe was standing to one side, with her helmet under her arm and her sunglasses on. When they got on the bikes at last, Emma had never been so grateful to feel her heart and legs working efficiently this time. Last year it had felt so hard, this year the kilometres flew by and she could even appreciate the scenery.

"This is great! It just feels so different."

"Well, you were pregnant you know!"

"True."

"How does it feel to have left little No-no at home?" Mikela couldn't really understand how Emma had been able to bring herself to leave such a little baby. On the other hand, she knew Emma.

"Don't call him that. But it's fine, Fred's on the case."

"One in a million, your Fred. Even with all his baggage." Mikela was beginning to feel a nesting instinct herself. She wouldn't mind having someone as dependable to come home to.

"His baggage doesn't bother me."

"What is he doing this summer?" Linda was curious.

"No idea. Didn't ask."

"You don't change, Emma." Chloe's face finally cracked into a grin as she started to get used to her girlfriends again. She had forgotten what it was like to be with people you loved, as opposed to rivals who were out to get you.

Luckily this conversation had taken place far from the microphone and camera as another part of the plan was for Julie to interview them all individually at various times. She would try and glean some of their backstories, their feelings about the others and their physical condition. All the usual 'how' questions. Emma wasn't sure what that was going to be like. She didn't want to be too harshly judged for leaving her baby behind, but it was so much part of why they were back. She realised she was going to have to try to keep the film crew on her side.

The first evening felt like a victory in itself. Against all the odds, they had been able to get back out there. Over a delicious local meal and a moderate amount of beer, they started to properly relax and remember what good friends they really were. Karl, Stephen and Julie blended in easily, although Karl was still filming and Julie was still asking probing questions. Stephen seemed to have been blinded by love or lust for Mikela. He followed her constantly with his eyes and, whenever possible, sat next to her.

Emma nudged Mikela as Stephen stood up to go to the bar again. "So?"

"He's lovely, but it's a bit sudden and risky right at the beginning of the trip, isn't it?

Emma smiled, she didn't think Mikela would hold out for too long.

"But you know, I quite fancy what you have, a nice little family, a nice comforting pair of arms to go home to."

"It sort of has its charms I suppose, but only if you make sure you have a means of getting away!"

"Well, you're here!"

"True!"

"So, girls, do you usually get any romantic interest on these trips?" Karl was mindful of his target audience. He needed some flesh, or flirting at the very least.

"Not really, well only Linda."

"Hey!"

"Well, we'll have to set something up, should be easy with a hot bunch of chicks like you." He raked them all with his eyes and laughed at their offended expressions. "Kidding!"

It was all quite intense. It was hot, either hot and windy or hot and humid. The terrain was sometimes difficult. Mikela and Stephen were falling hard for each other, but they hadn't made any moves yet. Karl kept doing embarrassing close-ups and encouraging them to chat to the young men he dragged along to the hotels every evening. Julie staged one interview a day. There was no time to think about anything else. Emma posted on Instagram whenever possible as usual, but she didn't pick up the phone to Fred.

Several evenings in, it was Emma's turn for the interview. It had been a long day. The crew had punctured and by all accounts, Karl had really lost it. They had been stuck for hours on a scorching dusty road and he decided to blame Julie for the fact that there was no spare tyre. She had been reduced to tears by his shouting. So, by the evening, Julie was not in a very accommodating mood.

"So, you and your man are having a break, are you?" That was her opening question and they got worse. Eventually Karl held up his hand.

"Stop Julie, that's enough. She's not the enemy." Emma snapped out of the rabbit in the headlights position she had been in.

"Damn right, you can leave me out of your horrible film if I get any more hassle like that."

"Hey." Karl was soothing. "We can't have the sexiest one in the group out of the picture." Julie had her fill of Karl for the day and stood up to leave. Unfortunately, there was no door to slam on the way out.

"I'll go and calm her down." Stephen was always the diplomatic, nice guy.

"So, Emma, are you on a break?"

"Hey, don't you start!" Karl held up his hands in surrender, "Look! No camera, purely personal interest." He tilted his head to check that she got his meaning. She did. "Let me get us a beer. We need one after all that."

Emma watched his back as he walked to the bar. He was exactly her type, tall, broad and confident. Was she on a break she wondered? Did it really matter what she did well away from home? But she would be putting a lot at risk, it would be wiser to stay rational.

Chapter Twenty-eight

Theo was excited, the competition season started in June and if he did well in the first ones, he would be able to up his game and enter the bigger ones. Added to that, he was moving in with Lotta. They wouldn't have to be in someone else's house, one of them always a guest, they would be a real, equal couple. He had even done well in his school work. He found it more interesting and relevant than the overly-explained, pedestrian-paced methods they followed at school. He was pretty sure of sailing through his Bac next year. And now Uncle J had added sugar to the churros by inviting his dad and the baby for the summer. Lucie had been messaging constantly with comments and photos of their baby brother. To be honest, he was a little jealous. He was amazed at himself, but seeing Lucie accept and love the baby so much, made him curious to get to know Noah. Even his mum seemed OK with the situation, which was frankly incredible.

Lotta hadn't pushed him on the subject. She had been living in this unconventional community on the beach for a while now. She had learnt how to accept situations in the here and now and to let go of the past and try not to worry about the future. So having a cute baby to share was a bonus, a potential source of joy, nothing more. Lotta herself, hadn't seen her dad for a long time. He had left for New Zealand with his new wife when she was only little. She did miss him though. This made Theo realise that he had nearly blown it with his own dad and he didn't want that. They had been super close before and he really wanted to get that back again. Who knew anyway, if his mum and dad spent the whole summer in the same house, anything might happen. He couldn't imagine that Emma (he had stopped calling her The Slut, even in his head, for the sake of little Noah) would be as good as gold surrounded by all those Incas or whoever.

He should stop that train of thought and go and do the evening yoga class. If you had told him a year ago that he would be into yoga in such a big way, he would never have believed it. But then again, it was the same for every single part of his life. Total change, 'hari nam'.

"Hey, Theo, coming to yoga?" Jaime had caught sight of the easily interpreted expressions on Theo's face.

"You read my mind, Jaime."

"I read your face, never play poker man, your face is an open book. Maybe you should grow a beard or something!"

"No need dude, my thoughts are all going to be irreproachable from now on. Namaste."

"Hey, a few tactics in a competition never went amiss."

"No worries, I can do that. Come on, let's go and get zenned."

"Is that a word?"

"It is now! Vamos!"

Jaime grabbed his mat and put his arm round Theo's shoulders. He was like the little brother he had never had, or a nephew perhaps, since he was with Theo's girlfriend's mother. Who cares, they were family. Uncle J, Caro, Lotta, Theo, they were strong, unbelievable. He hadn't had a conventional nuclear family growing up and this family of unrelated adults who had chosen each other, struck him as perfect. Caro was his ideal woman. He didn't know why he hadn't realised it before. Maybe it had taken Margot to make him realise that long term commitment was something worthwhile. It couldn't have worked between him and Margot, she was still in her marriage and he knew that, but he had no regrets. Caro had poured herself into his heart and filled up all the parts of him that he hadn't known were empty. She had turned him into a man, solid and consequential, and quite simply happy.

Caro was already lying on her mat when Theo and Jaime arrived, while Lotta looked after the last few customers in the bar. Her blond hair was spread out on her round ethnic print mat and she had her eyes closed. Her tall lithe body, already tanned nut-brown, radiated calm. To Jaime she looked incredibly inviting. It wasn't really yoga etiquette, but he couldn't help bending down to kiss her softly on the lips. Her blue eyes opened and her gently welcoming smile made him catch his breath. She winked at him, making him laugh.

"Yoga, Jaime, yoga!"

It was all so new, but it had all fallen into place like a chunky, wooden 3D puzzle. They fitted and formed a smooth whole. Theo missed his mum and dad, and even Lucie, not to mention Rufus, but there was no way he could imagine going back to his old life. He just hoped that karma wouldn't make him pay for those horrible compromising bits of fakery he had concocted before. He had to make sure he did as many good things as possible from now on, to counteract them.

The night that Margot, Fred, Lucie and Noah arrived in San Pere, Uncle J. had planned a welcome paella. It would be easy and convivial, after all the family had expanded. There were nine of them and he couldn't not invite Rafa if there was even the slightest hint of a celebration going on. Julian was revelling in his new life, life hadn't been bad before, but this happy mixture of people in his daily life was perfect. He only hoped that Fred would be cool. He was secretly looking forward to holding a baby in his arms again, he hadn't done enough of that in his life.

They might have been tetchy when they arrived after a long journey, but not at all. Noah was curious and fascinated. He clutched his dad, and held his arms out to Lucie while hiding his face from the others, but after a couple of smiles and peep-pos, he was a happy boy.

"He needs to roll on his tummy, Uncle J. That's what he likes best." Lucie was proud of her knowledge. Julian laughed and grabbed a throw from the sofa and creaked his way down onto it. "Show me!"

The sight of the round, tanned old man, bare foot in shorts and stick thin, blond-haired Lucie rolling from tummy to back on a rug made all of them howl with laughter. Noah copied them, laughing and rolling, grabbing the bits of Julian and Lucie that were within his reach. That was when Theo and Lotta turned up. Theo hugged his parents, who in turn hugged Lotta. Lucie jumped up.

"Here, Theo, take my place. He just loves rolling!"

Theo kissed his little sister on the cheek and lay down next to his great uncle and his new little half-brother. Noah stopped rolling in surprise and looked at him intently.

"Hello, bruv, how're you doing?" Theo gently stroked Noah's face and then suddenly rolled onto his back. Noah burst out laughing and followed suit.

Margot caught her breath at the physical resemblance between the two of them. She glanced at Fred to see if he had seen it. Whether or not he had, he was standing watching with a goofy grin and a glistening eye.

"Fred, help an old man up, will you?" Uncle J held his hand out. Fred hauled him up carefully, slapping him affectionately on the back as he did so.

"Less of the 'old' Uncle J, I have never seen you looking so hale and hearty. And something smells delicious, paella if I'm not mistaken."

"Indeed, indeed. Come and help me get some drinks sorted. Always happy to have an extra pair of hands."

And somehow that set the tone for the summer — easy, happy, fun. Noah was such a sunny baby. He had his fractious moments of course, usually because he had been over-entertained and needed some down time, which was reasonable and easy to understand. Margot seemed to remember Theo's bouts of distress being extreme and apparently random. They used to have to try everything to calm him down and then the next time that solution didn't work at all. But Noah was easy, a cuddle, a drink and a lay down in a shady cool spot and he sighed with relief and dropped off to sleep. Even better, the cuddle could come from any of them.

"He is such a good little boy, Fred." Margot had walked in to see Fred putting a just woken-up Noah into his bouncy chair.

"He is here, isn't he? Poor old Emma used to find him a handful at times you know."

"She must be really missing him, and you I suppose." 'What am I saying?' Margot caught herself, 'this is the immoral cow who broke up my family!'

"Back track Margot, I can read your thoughts... If I'm honest she only texts once a week and that is when I send her a photo of Noah. She says thanks and that's it."

Margot tried not to look too amazed, but it seemed incredible. She bent down and tickled Noah's tummy which had him chortling for more.

"As I was saying, Noah, you are so cute, aren't you?"

Fred looked over at his lovely wife, and she was still his wife. They had never made any official moves towards separating. His wife and his baby, who was not hers, and yet she was cooing at him with love. He really couldn't believe his luck and he really didn't deserve it. How was he supposed to resist her all summer?

Chapter Twenty-nine

Emma was wondering how Fred was managing on his own. She missed her little Noah, but when she felt like that she was hit by the memories of a screaming, red-faced inconsolable baby and the feelings of helplessness and despair which used to shroud her. She may not be attacking bonding issues or post-natal depression in a usual way, but she had been self-aware enough to know that she had to act. Maybe it was a bit radical and difficult to understand from the outside, but she felt a three month stretch of hard physical exercise, in a completely different place, was better for her than the same length of time in a mental hospital. Or worse, if things had got really bad, she might have done something really dreadful. She had a feeling that Fred had been worried about that too. So all in all, it had been a wise choice. And it was great. She was loving it in a way that she hadn't been able to last year, so really it was fair.

The same reasoning stopped her asking Fred where they were and how he was coping. It had to be a real break or it wouldn't work. If she started worrying about the niggling details of daily life on the other side of the planet, she wouldn't get the benefits from the trip she was hoping for. It seemed best to keep communication to a minimum.

"Penny for them..." Karl sat down next to Emma with a cool beer in each hand. She was sitting in the hotel bar, pleasantly tired after a day on the road. A photo of Noah had just pinged through with the briefest of messages from Fred saying they were both fine. There was no background to the photo, just a close up of her baby smiling up from his bouncy chair, which is what had started off her train of thought. She had no intention of sharing that with Karl.

"Not really thinking about anything. Just enjoying a nice cushioned seat, my beer and not listening to Mikela and Linda burble on."

"They are pretty chatty those two."

"They're lovely, but sometimes I need a moment on my own."

"Should I go?" Karl was already stretching out for his beer and starting to stand.

"No, no. It's fine. I've had my little think. Tell me how your day went."

And so, they settled into easy conversation. He made her laugh and he also made her feel singled out. He didn't hold back with compliments and he was a tactile kind of bloke. Quite naturally, they reinforced any points they made by touching each other's forearms. Emma punched him in the shoulder when he teased her and then he sat back with his arms sprawled along the back of the bench seat behind, close enough for their thighs to be almost touching. Emma was enjoying it, she had always loved this part, the anticipation, the manoeuvres, didn't everyone?

Karl was pretty sure he was reading her quite well. She knew the moves, she'd obviously played this game many times before, but on the other hand he knew about her home situation. Her baby was still very small, still he had time on this side, he was going to enjoy his stealthy stalking.

Mikela, on the other hand, was in love. Stephen was perfect. She couldn't believe quite how perfect he was. They were trying to underplay things in public for the sake of the trip and especially for the sake of the film. For one thing, if the others realised how they felt they might very quickly be elevated to being the prime romantic interest of the film. If there was one thing Mikela was keen to avoid, it was being filmed too often. Keeping it secret wasn't easy as neither of them could keep their eyes of the other. Stephen was a big man and he made her feel the perfect size for the first time in her life. In an extraordinary coincidence, they found that they lived within thirty kilometres of each other and then the clincher, they discovered they had the same birthday. So Mikela was in a love haze, she was imagining their babies, telling her granny she was getting married, planning the menu for their wedding. All this and they weren't even officially a couple. It was complicated because they all shared big rooms and they never had a room on their own. It was going to have to come out into the open soon, Stephen had told Mikela that he needed everyone to know they were in love. It was really like a dream, luckily it gave her the energy she needed to cycle. Even Chloe was impressed.

Julie had approached Linda, like Karl, she had a fair amount of experience in reality telly and she could tell who really wanted their time in the limelight. Linda had all the hallmarks of a perfect candidate, she was confident in her looks, groomed, attention seeking, feisty, with a slight edge of ruthlessness to spice up her niceness. Julie needed to find her accomplice who would make half the audience drool and the other half tut.

"So, Linda, unless you are thinking of hooking up with either Emma or Mikela, which it has to be said, would work, we need to find you a man." Linda spluttered into her beer.

"Seriously, we need some shots of you with a dangerous, Latin lover type…"

"Seriously? Are you joking? What kind of film are you making?"

"Hey, you know the score. Just a couple of shots of you drinking cocktails or you know, the old cold beer with the condensation dripping down your front. Nothing tricky."

"Good grief!" Linda tried to look shocked, but Julia could see that the idea had taken hold.

"Who's going to find this fantasy man then?"

"Well, I thought you were the one with the reputation!"

"Thanks a lot! Tell you what, you come out with me later and we'll see who we can find."

Julie raised her eyebrows and lifted her glass, "You're on!"

That evening there was only Emma and Chloe left in the hotel. Karl had gone with Julie and Linda in case there was something worth filming and Mikela and Stephen had disappeared. It was unusual for Chloe and Emma to talk in private, they were friends, but not intimate.

"Are you enjoying this, Chloe?"

"Actually, I really am. I needed a break. Competitive cycling is pretty intense, and I am pretty intense already, so…"

Emma nodded, "So it makes for too much tension and the risk of snapping, like a muscle or a tendon?"

"Exactly, maybe even literally." Chloe nodded, relieved to be talking about how she felt, "You too, no?"

"You're right, I was getting to the end of my tether. I was afraid of what I might do. I really adore Noah, but I'm not made to be a mum."

"There are lots of different types of mums, Emma, and you can't say one is better than the other. Maybe you need to be easier on yourself."

"Thanks, Chloe. You too, you know how amazing it is that you've done so well, don't you? You're like, in the top twenty female cyclists in France. That's amazing. You don't have to be number one to be proud of yourself."

"I know, logically, but tell that to my competitive spirit. You know it is really impressive that you are doing this trip so soon after having a baby, don't you? When you tell Noah when he is older, he'll be proud of his adventurous mummy."

"Or he'll hate me! What are we like? We need to learn from Linda and Mikela and take life as it comes a bit more."

"Let's see what state they are in when they get back before we decide to make them our role models, shall we?"

Emma laughed. "You're right, let's just have another beer and plan tomorrow."

Unsurprisingly they didn't see the others before they went to bed. The next morning Emma was up early, enjoying breakfast outside. The gentle early sun in the brightly coloured flowery courtyard at the back of the hotel was perfect. She leant back in her chair and lifted her face to the sun with her eyes closed appreciating the peace. Suddenly she felt a kiss on her lips.

"What the…"

"Sorry, couldn't resist." Karl smiled and kissed her again. For a brief moment Emma kissed him back before pushing him away.

"Hey! It's breakfast time, have a coffee." Emma smiled, determined to show it all meant nothing, hiding the fact that it had felt surprisingly good. "How did it go last night?"

"Oh, you know, the 3 Rs."

"Riotous, ribald and right out-of-it?"

Karl snorted, "Actually I was meaning raucous, random and…"

"Randy?" Emma guessed.

"Yup! Good footage though!"

"No broken hearts or noses?"

"Don't think so, I dragged them both home before it all got out of hand."

"What a gentleman!"

"I know, it's a hidden side of me, you haven't yet discovered. One of many!" He winked.

Fortunately, at that moment, Chloe arrived, followed closely by Mikela, a bubbly Linda and a distinctly green Julie.

"Good night, Julie?"

"Your friend is impressive." Julie held her head in both hands. Linda flicked her hair behind her shoulders and nodded.

"I really am!"

Mikela and Emma both threw their serviettes at her laughing. Chloe looked worried.

"I need to see the final rushes of that film before it goes out."

"It'll be fine, Chloe." Karl was reassuring. "We are aiming for a Sunday afternoon armchair public, so don't worry."

Just then Stephen strolled in looking sheepishly smug.

"Don't believe a word he says girls. Demand your rights! What have you been up to now, Karl?"

"Hey man! Right back at you. But it's not me, it's Miss JuJu here, she's been led astray by this lady."

"Aah, you see, he called me a lady, so it's all good. Pass me the jam, Mikela." With that Linda dipped her finger in her coffee and sucked it off suggestively.

"Here's the jam, honey. Now let's get going, rendezvous

in ten!"

"Well, I'm thanking my lucky stars that I'm a driver and not a rider this morning, although, Stephen, my most excellent, esteemed, friend, do you think you could..."

"Give me those keys, Julie, you must be still well over the limit. There's a little purple haze hanging over you. Don't anybody light a match!"

"Thanks, Stephen." Julie didn't even have the strength to defend herself. Mikela put her arms round her shoulders sympathetically.

"Have another empanada, I've been where you are now. A night out with Linda needs careful preparation and training. Good job Karl was with you."

Julie just shook her head and the others all burst out laughing.

Chapter Thirty

Theo and Lotta had slipped seamlessly into their new life together. Somehow, they just found it easy. They had both been used to busy lives and they were both surprisingly tidy. Living where they worked helped, it meant they were never late. They both had school work to do as well as their jobs and training. And they were simply happy and in love. Theo was really happy to have the rest of his real family around, as well as his new family. He felt much more mellow towards his dad and he had fallen under Noah's spell like everyone else. The role of Very Big Brother was a nice one to have. He had enough distance and objectivity now to see that his dad had suffered almost as much as his mum for a stupid mistake. He could see now that he himself had helped create an unresolvable situation. He hadn't completely white-washed his dad, but he wanted to clear the air between them. It felt like a good old clichéd man-to-man conversation might be possible. He was building up to it. Soon.

One Thursday Uncle J suddenly announced he was going away for the weekend.

"Every year I go and see my dear friend Isabella for three days. Three days is perfect, any more and we fight. So I'll get the train tomorrow." He announced his news over the dinner table to the surprised expressions of the others.

"Is Isabella an old girlfriend, Uncle J?" asked Lucie.

"Well Lucie, she's old and she's my girlfriend, so I

suppose so."

"You see your girlfriend once a year?" Lucie looked astonished.

"No Lucie, twice a year. It's good! It suits us both. We WhatsApp too!"

"You kept that a secret, Uncle J." Margot felt almost hurt that she hadn't known before.

"Not a secret, just hadn't mentioned her, you know how it is." He winked at Margot which troubled Fred, what other unmentionables were there as yet untold? "So, I'll see you all on Sunday evening."

"Well not me, I going to stay at the stables on Saturday and Sunday night with Inés. Her parents are away and she needs some company. The grooms are there though, so no need to worry."

Fred and Margot just nodded, feeling slightly ineffectual.

Which all meant that on Saturday there was only Margot and Fred, and of course Noah, at the villa. There was a kite-surf competition an hour up the coast and Caro and Lotta had gone to watch their men compete. Margot hadn't wanted to go so far away, just in case Lucie needed her.

It was a beautiful, calm, balmy evening. Margot was playing with Noah on the sofa on the terrace and Fred sat down next to them. The tension between them had almost completely evaporated over the last few weeks as they shared their lives and looking after their family. As Noah calmed and snuggled into a sleeping position in Margot's arms, Fred put his arm around her.

"Thanks for everything, Margot. I am so lucky." And he kissed her. It was familiar, but new. The connection was still there. Fred pulled back and looked at Margot. She was pink through her tan and her eyes told him that she had felt it too.

He got to his feet and gently took the baby and then pulled her to her feet. Holding Margot by the hand he took Noah through to his cot and put him down. Both arms free, he kissed Margot again with an intensity and passion he had forgotten existed. And she responded. She could feel his love and his need and right here, right now, that was what she wanted too.

When they woke the next morning to the sound of Noah's bells on the inside of his cot, they realised that he had slept through the night. Fred went to pick him up and quite naturally put him between the two of them in the bed. Margot had a sudden realisation of how wrong it must be.

"Is this OK do you think?" She grabbed the sheet a bit tighter.

"He's not going to tell anyone and he doesn't look traumatised." Fred smiled and pushed her hair off her face.

"True, he doesn't. I must stop being so suburban."

"You are anything but suburban, you are a glorious, yet brainy surf-babe!" Fred was trying to pull the sheet down to get a better look at her breasts.

"Stop it Fred, behave." She didn't sound convincing. Last night had made her remember how much she liked how they were together and her body was treacherously screaming for more. "Go and get your poor baby his bottle. You're hungry aren't you, Noah?"

Fred did, but not before coming round to her side of the bed and kissing her, slipping his hand under the cover as he did so. Fortunately, Noah wasn't desperately hungry.

Although both of them would dearly loved to have simply slipped back into their marriage, to walk down to the beach holding hands, to just be together again, it was impossible.

There was a baby and a great big elephant in the room. So they stayed at the villa that morning, prepared a simple lunch and delayed the inevitable for as long as possible. But dishes done, Noah down for his nap, they had to face the situation.

"We can't confuse the kids with all this. You have to decide what you want, Fred. So do I. It's not simple. I can't even work out what the honourable thing to do is." Margot reached out for Fred's hand.

"I know, I mean, I know what I want, but I can't see how it's possible."

"What do you want, Fred?"

"I want this of course." Fred swept his arm indicating everything. "I want you, to live with you as my wife, but with Noah too."

"And Emma?"

"I know."

"I'm going to act completely out-of-character. We need to think things through, both of us, before doing anything at all, but first, could we just go back to bed while Noah's asleep?"

Fred's mouth fell open in surprise. "Hell, yes! Come here wife!"

She did.

By chance, Theo turned up mid-afternoon hoping to have a heart to heart with his dad. He had done really well in the competition, he'd come second and the party afterwards had been great. They had all slept around the campfire and driven back not long after day-break. Caro and Jaime had their businesses to take care of and Lotta was windsurfing with her friends. His slight hang-over had dissipated and he was looking forward to basking in some parental praise.

The garden of the villa was unusually empty, but Theo

realised that Noah must be having his nap. He stood listening, but then he suddenly realised what he was listening to and he retraced his steps quickly. He hurried back to the bar, willing himself not to jump to any conclusions nor to over-react.

"Lotta, have you seen my mum?"

"No, Theo, nor your dad." Theo shook his head. "What's the matter?"

"Nothing, just wanted a chat with Dad. It's just…"

"What? Are you OK? You look pale. Too many beers last night?"

"It's not that, it's Mum and Dad, they're…"

Lotta ran round from behind the bar and grabbed Theo into a hug, effectively silencing him. "Don't say any more, Theo, just leave them to sort things out. Don't even think anything." And she kissed him hard, she was happy about the potential non-mentionable news as well.

"I love you, Lotta Janssen, you are my guardian angel."

"Not so much of the angel. Why don't we go home and play mummies and daddies!"

Theo chuckled and lifted her into his arms to carry her ostentatiously across the fifty metres of beach to their little flat above the kite surf office, acknowledging all the comments and smiles from the regular beach-goers with a triumphant grin.

Margot was reeling. She really hadn't expected the weekend to turn out like it had. She knew in her heart of hearts that Fred still loved her and she knew that deep down she still loved him. What surprised her was that she had managed to get past what he had done. What worried her was that she was having some kind of revenge on Emma. Then again, it had been so much more than she could have even imagined. It was as though they had both been liberated, or been taught a new trick or two. That seemed all wrong though. And little Noah, he might love his Tata Margot, but he needed his mum. What a mess. At least no one else knew, maybe the best thing would be to just forget it happened.

Theo and Lucie had adjusted to the separation, family relations were all on a good footing. The most sensible thing would be to think of it as a mistake and continue as before. That, of course, meant that she couldn't discuss it with anybody. She could have talked to Jaime, but now he was with Caro and he was too close to Theo. She dreaded to think what Jan would have to say, she would rather not know. And there was also the small fact that it hadn't felt like a mistake at all.

"Fred, we need to think things through and we need a couple of hours apart before Uncle J. gets back and guesses. Go for a run. I'll look after Noah."

"I'll only be able to manage a jog, love, but you're right. We need to think. Don't you want to kite-surf?"

"I think I'd drown, you go, nobody will be watching you."

"You're right as usual. I'll see you in a bit."

So, Margot settled down to a couple of hours of baby-sitting. She strapped Noah into his buggy and called Rufus. She could pick up some groceries and have a coffee at Caro's. In spite of what she had said to Fred, she wanted to avoid thinking, if at all possible. Anyway, it was hardly her role in all this to be proactive, canny perhaps, but no more.

Theo and Lotta decided to go and have a drink at the villa. They had no food left and were hoping for an invite to stay to eat. If they were honest, they wanted to see how things were. When they got there, there was only Margot and Noah, but Fred arrived back soon after, sweaty from his run. Theo glanced at Lotta wondering how she read the situation, but she just shook her head slightly.

As Fred emerged from the shower to join them for a drink, Uncle J's battered old jeep arrived in a cloud of dust. Both doors opened and, to everyone's surprise, a lady of a certain age came round from the passenger's side. She had long curly silver hair which was held back by big turtle shell combs from a lived-in, deep brown, smiling face. Her bright red skirt swished as she walked, her bare shoulders still straight.

"Hola!" She smiled confidently at them all.

"Everybody, this is Isabella. I've told her so much about you all that she had to come and meet you. Normally she doesn't come here, but now, well, we said, why not?"

"Hello, hello one and all! Theo, hola! Lotta, and you must be the infamous Fred, and of course Julian's beloved Margot."

They all shook hands, taken aback. Noah gurgled and kicked from his position on the floor. Isabella crouched down to tickle his tummy.

"And Noah. Hola niño."

Uncle J sat down in his spot and smiled benevolently at them all.

"Isabella is going to stay for a few nights." Julian saw Margot's face and pre-empted her question.

"Don't worry, she sleeps with me!"

They were all guilty of looking slightly shocked and trying to cover it up. Isabella laughed.

"Of course, you may not be aware of it, but Julian and I have been lovers for over sixty years, just never in this house."

"Well, there was once…"

"Oh true, but that's why I didn't come back, querido."

Margot was busy wondering where Donna fitted into this story. Theo with the bluntness of youth, didn't hold back.

"Sixty years! Amazing, how come we didn't know?"

"Too complicated to explain, but no reasons not to any more, eh Julian?" Isabella smiled. Lotta nudged Theo, wanting him to stop asking questions.

"Anybody for a drink?" Fred was keen to change the subject and also gasping for some alcohol.

The evening went well, Julian and Isabella were funny together and Fred and Margot were relieved not to have the spotlight on them. Theo was just happy with his lovely Lotta, his success of the day before and his hopes for his parents, not to mention his respect for his old dog of a great uncle.

Chapter Thirty-one

When Lucie got back the next day, there was a change in the atmosphere at the villa. She dropped her bike at the gate and bounded onto the terrace. She did an almost cartoon like screech to a halt when she saw Julian sitting next to Isabella on the old sofa, holding hands.

"Hola! Me llamo Lucie."

"Hi Lucie, I'm your Uncle J's secret lover." Lucie blushed, Isabella just cackled.

"Isabella, behave! Poor Lucie." Julian tutted, still smiling. Lucie skipped forward and kissed her great uncle on the cheek and shyly held out her hand to Isabella. Isabella pulled her towards her and planted a big kiss on Lucie's cheek.

"Tell me about Manté, when can I see him?"

"You know about Manté?"

"Of course, your Uncle J tells me everything about his lovely little great niece."

Lucie was won over. "Where are Mum and Dad?"

"They're down at the beach with Noah and Rufus. Shall we all walk down. A quick dip would be just the ticket, what do you think, Isa?"

"I am up for anything!"

The summer trundled on, Isabella only stayed for five nights, but it was still more than her allotted three. On her last night, they all ate together.

"It's been lovely, amigos, but with Julian and I, the secret of our longevity has been to keep things fresh. Too much time together could dampen the spark, but I'll be back. Here's to the rest of your summer." Inspired by her optimism, they all raised their glasses to that.

Isabella had filled the house with her personality, colourful clothes and lack of inhibitions. Fred and Margot had gratefully retreated into the background. The noise and party atmosphere had covered their quietness. Margot was relieved to be able to avoid thinking too much. The wind was perfect, so she took advantage of it. Fred was kite-surfing passably well by now, but he still needed the easier early winds, so Margot looked after Noah, going out after him when the winds had picked up. Physical tiredness helped them to sleep and the whirlwind that Isabella had created helped distract them from their feelings. Fred couldn't help squeezing her hand sometimes and neither of them could help looking after each other. Fred couldn't see a way forward, he was stuck in a mess of his own making.

Theo was still keeping an eye on his dad when he was kite-surfing, giving him tips and occasionally rescuing him with the boat. After one of the more epic rescues, they were sitting on the sand in front of the surf hut with a bottle of beer each, when Theo felt the time was right.

"Dad, I'm so sorry for what I did. It feels like it was somebody else. I mean, I know I did it, but I can't believe I was so stupid and naive. I really messed things up for you and Mum."

Fred put his arm around his son, "It was me who messed up, son, not you. You had every right to be angry. I was stupid, so stupid. It would have spoiled things between me and your mum whatever. It might have been less embarrassing, but she would have known somehow. At least we don't have any secrets now."

"Like Uncle J!"

"Yes, what about that hey? I'm not made for secrets and stuff. You know I had to make Emma my 'girlfriend' because the principal at school insisted, don't you?"

"Dad! You've had a baby with her since then."

"God, you're right. I'm making excuses again. But you must know that Noah wasn't planned. I love him and I've loved him since the very first instance that I knew of his existence, but it wasn't what I had in mind."

"Should it be me giving you the talk about contraception, Dad?" Theo laughed, "Seriously though, Noah is great. You know what I've discovered on this beach? Labels, official relationships don't matter at all. It's who you choose to love and care for who are your family. Having the same DNA only counts for so much."

"So wise, so young. You're right though. Your mum and I were each other's family from the first time we kissed."

"And now?" Theo looked at his dad knowingly. Fred just shook his head.

"We'll just have to wait and see Theo. I just don't know what'll happen. I'll answer any question, I owe you that, but I think I'd rather you didn't ask them." They clinked bottles and drank the beer which tasted of Spain and male bonding. "Theo, I love you and I'm so glad we talked. I'm very, very proud of you and as part of the new me, I want you to know." They clinked again.

"Thanks, Dad, love you too."

That was the last peaceful moment they had for a while. Shortly afterwards, an inevitably wet and sandy Rufus jumped on them both excitedly, followed by a laughing Lucie. Rufus wanted to play, and he was being unusually persistent. He was leaping from side to side, landing with his bottom in the air and his chin on his paws. Soon they were all diving and jumping in the sand and then in the shallow waves, having pure, unadulterated fun.

Lucie was running onto the beach to escape another dunking when she saw her mum approach. Margot waved and Lucie carried on running, intending to use her as a shield from the men in her family. But then she saw her mum's face and stopped.

"What's the matter? Where's Noah?"

"Well, bit of a surprise, Emma is here."

"Emma? Oh, get off Rufus." Rufus did not care about unusual visitors, he just wanted everyone in his game. Fred and Theo were just behind him.

"What's up?"

"Emma's here, Dad." Lucie watched her dad's face intently, reading his reaction.

"I nearly didn't recognise her, she's had her hair cut really, really, short, and it is so blond, it's white." Margot knew she was being inconsequential. "Anyway, I left her with Noah obviously, and Uncle J, and came to get you." She looked at Fred, unable to hide the pain in her eyes. She had been kidding herself, thinking she was coping, she wasn't. As soon as she had seen those long brown legs twist out of the door of the taxi, she knew she'd been praying for her never to come back.

"Gosh, I'd better go then." Fred was stunned. He had read in Margot's face the answers to all the questions he'd been asking himself and all he wanted to do was to gather her into his arms, but he couldn't. He had to be tidier, to sort things out.

"I'll see you all in a bit."

Rufus shook himself, soaking Margot, which helpfully lightened the atmosphere.

"Do you think she'll take Noah away, Mum?" Lucie looked stricken.

"I don't know, Lucie, I don't know anything at all."

Theo stepped in to help his mum, "Let's go and grab a drink at Caro's, give them a bit of time to get sorted."

Emma had got out of the taxi and taken a deep breath. It had been a long journey on top of a really long flight the day before. She had arrived home, dying to see her baby and Fred and there had been no one there. It was obvious that the flat had been shut up for weeks. There were cobwebs in the sink and the one plant that someone had inadvisably given her for her birthday, had died. She was tired, hungry and annoyed. There was next to nothing in the fridge and no cries of joy at the sight of her. She also felt slightly guilty that she didn't know where they were, she should have shown more interest. She unearthed a bottle of wine, poured herself a glass and sat down to think.

She could hardly blame Fred for not hanging around just in case she showed up, she was going to have to turn over a new leaf and be more caring, less selfish. Her trip away had been necessary, she had been on the edge of disaster, but things would be better now. Well, they would be as soon as she could locate them. Nobody could hide easily these days though. She logged onto Facebook and sure enough, a few clicks later, there was a picture of her baby in the arms of his step-sister, beach, sea and kite-surfs in the background. Fred had simply taken Noah to join his old family. Had they all, even Margot, just taken them in? It hardly seemed possible. And she'd been feeling guilty about her trip, definitely not any more. Finding the address of the villa might have proved more complicated as she didn't know Julian's surname, but she had a stroke of luck. She was glancing through a pile of letters and papers on the kitchen table, when she found it written on a post-it. It was an address in San Pere Pescador anyway, it had to be the right one. She stuck her clothes on a quick wash, had another glass of wine and booked a flight. She'd have to get taxis to and from the airport, but she would be there by mid-afternoon.

When Fred pushed the gate open, he was greeted by the sight of Emma lying nose-to-nose with Noah who was trying to grab her dangly earrings. Julian was nowhere to be seen.

"Emma, hi! You're back, you found us!" He sounded falsely cheerful to his own ears. Emma stood up slowly and took a step towards him.

"I'm back, yes. I didn't expect you to be here." Fred nodded, but said nothing. "How long have you been here?"

"Oh, since halfway through July."

"Really? Here? In this house?"

"Yep, there's room, Theo moved in with Lotta."

"And your wife?"

"She's here too, of course."

"I know, I saw her. She looks very different."

"Funny, that's what she said about you…" Emma ran her hand over her velvety buzz cut. She thought she looked pretty edgy with it and it was great under a helmet. Karl had called it sexy as hell, Fred seemed almost disgusted.

"Did Noah recognise you?" Fred asked.

"Of course he recognised his mummy, didn't you, little one?" Noah looked back at her with interest.

Fred was flummoxed, he couldn't think straight. Emma

didn't seem to have any issues with the awkwardness of the situation.

"Well, I could do with a bit of lazing on a beach, it was a long trip. Presumably you have a double bed?"

At that moment Uncle J, who may or may not have been eavesdropping from the kitchen, walked out to the terrace with a jug of lemonade in his hand.

"Fred has a double bed, my dear, and Noah has a cot in his room. You are welcome to stay." Fred glared at Julian, but he could see that it was the only rational thing to do. Or they could all leave, maybe that would be better. He begged his brain to speed up and find a solution. Too late!

"Great, thanks a lot! Cheers!" Emma held up her glass of lemonade in a toast as though staying with her boyfriend's ex's family was the most natural thing in the world. Fred sighed and bent down to pick up Noah. At least Noah should be happy with the arrangement.

"He needs changing, don't you, wee lad? Do you want to do it, Emma?"

"No, you do it, I'm whacked from my travels." Fred nodded again, it seemed to be all he was capable of. At least he could text the others to warn them that their new guest would be staying. He hoped Lucie wouldn't be too mad. Or Margot too sad. Oh god!

That evening meal was the strangest they had had yet. Uncle J had insisted that Caro, Jaime, Rafa, his masseur and a couple of the kite instructors joined them, as well as Theo and Lotta obviously. So it was noisy and boisterous. Emma was full of her adventure, encouraged by the young surfers who were planning a trip to South America for the winter. Fred was finding it quite hard to even look at her with her skull-like head.

Lucie was safely tucked between Uncle J and Lotta, saying very little. Margot was silent too, she had put on her flicky skirt, a simple black top and let her hair loose to give herself confidence, but she couldn't talk normally. The rest of them did their best to keep things as upbeat and civilised as possible. Eventually the guests left, Lucie had slipped away earlier. Emma stood up and held out her hand to pull Fred up.

"Come on Fred, let's go to bed." What else could he do?

Chapter Thirty-two

A new chapter in their lives started. Margot spent more time doing sport and with Uncle J as she wasn't babysitting any more. She missed her time alone with little Noah, but she had to have some limits. There was a competition coming up and Jaime had persuaded her to enter which was a nice distraction. Kite-surfing was so intense that it emptied the mind of anything else which was exactly what she needed.

Emma was a big hit on the beach, with her long perfect limbs, androgynous hair and to Fred's surprise and horror, a new huge pair of wings tattooed on her back. Unfortunately, she wasn't such a hit with Noah. She tensed when she picked him up and he felt it. She was still expecting the incessant crying and it was as though Noah didn't want to disappoint her.

One afternoon, when she had been in charge of Noah since lunchtime, he had woken up from his nap grumpily after only twenty minutes. He normally slept for an hour or so after lunch, but now he was hot and unrested and he was complaining. Emma was instantly thrown back to the feelings of desperation that she used to have. She picked him up and bounced him up and down, but it just made things worse. There was no one else around, Margot and Julian had gone shopping, Lucie was at the stables and Fred was kite-surfing. Noah just kept crying. Emma had to find help; she was worried she would hurt him. Eventually she ran to the bar hoping to find Caro. She thrust the red, snotty little boy into Caro's surprised arms.

"What's the matter, Noah? Emma? What's wrong?"

"I can't do it. He won't shut up." Noah had already calmed down. With the odd little remaining sob, he took the piece of bread Caro was offering him.

"It's just his teeth, Emma."

"But how do you know that? I never know what to do." Privately Caro thought that if Emma spent a little bit more time with her baby and had not left him for three months, then she would know what to do, but she could hardly say that.

"You'll get the hang of it soon. He loves his mama."

"I don't think he does. He loves you more than me." Caro just shook her head and used her free arm to make Emma a cup of tea.

"Drink this, smile, look happy, he'll smile. All kids love their mums." Emma tried, she could understand that a baby would prefer to be with a happy person, so she tried to be positive and shake his stupid rattles for him like she saw Lucie do for hours. It just didn't seem to be part of her make-up. And then the same thing happened again two days later. This time she didn't feel she could go to Caro. She had been nice to her, but she had sensed an underlying disapproval. She would have to dig deep. She tried everything, bread, biscuits, he spat them out with disgust. His rattle, his teddy, he threw them hard back at her. He was rearing back away from her as she tried to comfort him when, bang, he crashed his head onto the bridge of her nose. It really hurt.

"God, you little bastard." She flung him down on the sofa. His head bounced and he was crying more than seemed possible.

At that moment Margot jumped out of the jeep and ran through the gate. She grabbed Noah who was just about to fall off the sofa and held him tight. He looked at her with big watery eyes and grabbed hold of her hair as if he would never let go.

"Emma, are you OK?" Margot had never addressed her directly before, but this was clearly a crisis. Emma had blood streaming from her nose. Uncle J was close behind, holding out his clean, white, omnipresent hanky. Emma was in tears now too. She looked like the victim of some kind of natural disaster, blood splattered, too thin with wild reddened eyes and a big red mark on the bridge of her nose. Julian gently made her sit down and stem the blood, keeping a large comforting hand on her shoulder.

Margot took Noah to the bathroom to cool him down and change his very dirty nappy. She laid him gently on his changing mat and he finally let go off her hair and smiled at her. She caught sight of his new tooth and congratulated him on it, rubbing his tummy and then his toes. Ten minutes later, he was his normal sunny self and she was just emerging back onto the terrace with him, when Fred came home.

Fred saw Margot and Noah first, they were happy and smiling, and then Julian handing a destroyed Emma a glass of water. He couldn't make sense of it.

"Fred, there was a little accident and Emma had a nose bleed. And look, Noah has a new tooth!" Margot was desperate to diffuse the situation, it was unbearable. She handed Fred his baby. Emma stared at them and realised what she had been too blind to see before. They were a couple. She might be sleeping with Fred, but he and Margot were together. One last sob shuddered through her body, her nose bleed dried up and her resolve picked itself up.

"I need a shower. Won't be long." She needed time to

decide on a plan and to work out what she wanted. Maybe she could have it all.

From then on Emma found she didn't have to cope with Noah on her own. There always seemed to be someone around. She didn't care if they didn't trust her to look after her own baby, it suited her. On top of that, she had some news from Linda. The film was going to be finished soon. They were planning a party with a private viewing in a week's time. There would still be a bit of post-production to do after that, but they would get a good idea of how it would look. Emma felt a flush of excitement, a glamorous party, away from all this clannish domesticity, Karl. She booked a flight. Then she told Fred.

"Emma, this has got to stop. You have to talk to me first, include me in your plans. What if I had something on that weekend, what would you plan for Noah then?"

"Come on, Fred. Anybody here will look after him."

"You're his mother."

"He doesn't like me." Emma hissed. Fred was shocked into silence. He felt suddenly and desperately sorry for her. Yes, she was gorgeous, if she would grow her hair back anyway, sexually insatiable and could be great fun, but sadly and irredeemably, she just didn't get human relationships. He was still worried though. She might still try and take Noah away from him, he couldn't just end their affair. He couldn't bear the thought of Noah being passed backwards and forwards or not seeing him for days on end. His absolute priority was to be a full-time dad for Noah.

"OK, I suppose you're right in a way. You'll have a nice time."

She did.

Chapter Thirty-three

Margot had been profoundly shocked by the scene she had come back to. She hadn't realised how bad things had got for Emma. She obviously had some deep-rooted issues, equally obvious was that Margot herself, was not the person to help. Another realisation, which had hit her like a blow from a sledgehammer, was just how attached she had become to Noah. Seeing him at risk like that had brought all her maternal feelings to the fore. She organised things so that Emma wasn't alone with Noah. Fred hadn't expressed his fears about Emma taking Noah away, but it was pretty clear to Margot what his worries were. And she shared them. As a health professional, she had seen some hideous cases of bitter wrangling over custody and the effects on the children involved could be heart-breaking. They had to avoid that at all costs. It was possible that Emma was still suffering from post-natal depression, but whatever the trigger, she needed help coming to terms with her role as a mother. Margot wouldn't have minded a little help and advice herself.

Then suddenly, Lucie had her first human crush. It was so classic that it was almost funny. Her friend at the riding school had her cousins to stay for August and one of them was a year older than Lucie with the dark hair, eyes and skin of a typical Spaniard. Apparently, he was an excellent rider, played the guitar and was sweetly gallant to his cousin and her friend. Lucie was off her food, spent hours in the bathroom and scribbling Lucie Caballero on bits of paper in her bedroom. She mentioned Antonio's name every other sentence until suddenly she didn't mention it at all any more. Margot's instinct told her that something had moved on in their friendship. On one hand, Margot was relieved that Lucie seemed to have got over her disgust at the base nature of all males, but on the other she didn't want her to suffer from it. Of course, she knew she couldn't do much really. Lucie would have to learn her own lessons, but a little conversation about self-preservation, contraception and vaccination was definitely called for. She still had her own parenting to do.

"When is your next demo with Manté, Lucie?"

"This Thursday, why?"

"I haven't been for a couple of weeks, I love seeing you do your stuff." Lucie looked a bit shifty which strengthened Margot's resolve. Their little chat needed to be sooner rather than later.

Forty minutes of arduous parenting later, Margot made her way onto the terrace. She was dying for a large glass of wine. Lucie had wrung her out, she had swung from denial, to excessive defensive emotion, to finally a grudging acceptance that her mum might know, if not best, then at least a little. Margot knew the conversation was not over yet, but she had Lucie's permission to make her an appointment to see a doctor and get the ball rolling. Maybe another expression would be more appropriate, Margot smiled wryly at herself.

"Good to see you're still smiling." Fred appeared with two huge glasses of perfectly chilled white wine. "That sounded intense."

"You read my mind, thanks, Fred."

"Well actually I heard the beginning, so I was pretty sure

you would need one. Is Lucie OK?"

"She's fine, she's lovely, just completely head-over-heels, out-of-control, in love with Antonio. It'll be fine, I'm sure he's a nice lad and I can handle the technical side of things!"

Fred laughed, "You certainly know how to handle those, Margot! Here's to you being such a great mum. Cheers!"

Margot was moved. He had read things right, anticipated their needs and shown he cared. "You're a pretty good dad yourself. I'm so glad you sorted things with Theo too."

"Cheers to that, my love." It just slipped out. They both heard it, acknowledged it silently and let it go. "I'm looking forward to the show on Thursday."

The next day Fred was laying the table outside for their evening meal when a taxi drew up.

"Isabella, this is a surprise! Welcome, welcome!"

"Hello, young Fred. Is the hombre de mi vida around?"

"He'll be back in a few minutes. He just popped out to get some bread."

"Is there room for one more at your table?"

"Of course, shall I put your bag in your room?"

"We'd better check with J first."

"Even after sixty years?"

"Why do you think things are still so fresh after sixty years. Never, never presume young Fred, always make an effort, always woo."

"Woo, eh? Interesting word, much more gallant than flirt or seduce. It seems to imply honourable intent."

"Now there's an interesting concept, intent to do what though? Simply to love and respect I think, not to have and to hold or, heaven help us, honour and obey."

Fred burst out laughing, "So true, and all this wisdom

before you've even sat down. I think, this calls for mojitos."

"The very reason I planted that mint over there all those years ago. Where are all your women?"

"You get some mint, I'll fill you in on my…"

"Your what, Fred?" Margot had heard the last comment and was fearing the worst, but she was smiling and delighted to see Isabella.

"Margot, querida, you look lovelier than ever." The two women hugged and kissed.

"Fred, will you make a virgin mojito for Lucie please."

"I will while I can!" Fred winked as he headed for the kitchen.

"Fred!"

"Tell me all, Margot" Isabella was still holding her hand.

"Later Isabella, with pleasure." Margot sighed with relief at the thought of being able to talk things through with someone so non-judgmental, positive and wise. It was just what she needed.

When Julian got back with Rufus and some bread, the surprised grin with which he greeted Isabella was a pleasure to see. Then he kissed her long and hard. When they surfaced, Isabella winked at Fred, "Wooing, you can't beat it!"

On Thursday night, Fred, Margot, Uncle J and Isabella went to watch Lucie ride Manté. They arrived early so that Lucie could show Isabella the stables and so that the other three could take the opportunity to suss out the famous Antonio. They were all pleased and relieved when Lucie shyly introduced them. As the kids went back to their preparations, Fred heaved a sigh of relief.

"He's just a nice young boy, he won't hurt her." His shoulders relaxed, "I don't know what I imagined, but a boy is fine!"

"What did you expect?" Uncle J's eyes were twinkling with amusement.

"I think I was worried he might be some big hairy man!" They all laughed again.

The next day Julian and Isabella were sitting drinking coffee after breakfast.

"Isabella, are you sure you came to see me? I have a feeling you came to see my family. Or Margot, perhaps?"

"Now Julian, a little bit of jealousy, I like! You are your family anyway. I came for you of course, but you're right, Margot needs me."

"Do you think they can find a way out of the pickle they are in?"

"I hope so, look at us! If we can…"

Julian nodded, raising his eyebrows in agreement and gathering her to him for another long kiss. He really liked kissing and apparently it kept lips supple and full, so why deprive oneself?

It was funny, the first time any of them came across Uncle J and Isabella snogging on the sofa under the tree, they were a little shocked and very embarrassed, but it quickly became acceptable and even sweet. Who wanted a boring couple who sniped or even ignored each other? Theo summed it up eloquently, "Those two are really into each other."

They really were.

Chapter Thirty-four

"Margot, we need to talk about your marmalade." Isabella was having a milky coffee in the shade after breakfast and Margot was just coming back from yoga.

"My marmalade?" She looked quizzical.

"I think that's what Julian said, or was it jam? Oh no, wait, it was pickle. That's it, your pickle."

"My jam or my pickle? Ah, I see what you are getting at!"

"Some straight talking I think." Isabella put down her cup and looked stern.

Margot smiled and lowered herself into a deckchair.

"So, you love Fred, you love Noah and you find yourself feeling sorry for Emma." Margot's jaw dropped. Isabella was both perceptive and forthright. "Do you want him back? If so, on what terms, that's the question. How were things before? Is that what you want back? Was there wooing?" Margot smiled, the "wooing theory" was sweet and she could see the truth in it. "Maybe you could all simply have it all?"

"How would that work?" Margot was puzzled.

"Well, you are listening to an ageing hippy who got caught up in bourgeois rubbish, but couldn't you just share a bit?"

"Be his harem, like he was going to say the other day? No way!"

"No, no, but you could have your own freedom too. You had a little love with Jaime did you not? And it didn't do you any harm did it?"

"You think we could just be together when she's away and if she's home then I can hang out with whoever I like. What about the kids?"

"Well, what about the kids, what do you want them to have as a model? An illusion of happy ever after, or a real happy ever after?"

Margot was trying to be receptive, trying to imagine a future where anything went, but her mind kept stumbling over all the obstacles. What would Emma say? She didn't strike Margot as being a one-man girl, but still, would she just go off places knowing that Margot would be climbing into bed with Fred and mothering her child while she was gone? And where would they live? Here in this unconventional world on the beach, it might just be possible, but imagine at home. Parent's meetings. Neighbours. She shuddered. "It just couldn't work."

"Well, I think it could, you don't have a lot of choice, do you? Fred is the hombre de tu vida, you don't want to walk out of his life and I can see you don't want to be just friends either. Neither does he. Take it from one who knows, it might work."

"Is that your secret? To your wooing freshness?"

"A secret is just that, so…"

Margot gulped, trying to understand how Isabella and Julian had run their lives and feeling frankly naive. But then look how her life had changed in the last two years. There had been misery and despair, but from bland and boring, their lives had become vibrant and full. She shook her head. She supposed it was something to think about.

Later that afternoon, Margot and Fred found themselves alone with Noah. The wind was too strong for them to kite-surf and Julian had announced he was taking Isabella shoe shopping.

"Shoe shopping? Is that the secret to eternal love?" Fred was only half joking, it was obvious that Julian was doing something right.

"Well not for me! Actually, I have some inside information about those two!" And she told Fred the gist of Isabella's solution for the situation they were in.

"So a kind of ménage à trois with optional extras?"

"I thought it was going to be sister wives like the Mormons! I heard you think 'harem' the other day…" They both laughed, Noah joined in, happy in the relaxed afternoon calm of the little-used sitting room. Margot had livened up the décor in this room too and above all, thrown away some of the tatty junk which had been taking up so much house space for years. She'd done it tactfully and Uncle J had seemed genuinely pleased. Now it looked cheerful and clean, still beachy, but cosy too.

"Seriously, Margot, since we're talking. I don't know how we can continue like this. You know I want you and love you more than ever, but I can't take any risks with this little one." He blew a raspberry in Noah's irresistible squidgy tummy to hide his stress.

"Fred, I know. I mean I know you, I usually know what you're thinking. We could learn the art of wooing without resorting to third parties, couldn't we?"

"I would never take anything for granted again. If possible, I would take you shoe shopping every day for the rest of our lives."

"In the spirit of honest confession, no thanks, but I love you too, Fred. I tried to stop, but it didn't work. And a bit on the side now and then seems like an attractive idea, but it would also seem too messily risky or riskily messy. Not sure which." They were laughing again. They were declaring serious grown-up love to each other and they could still make each other laugh.

"Also, by the way, it makes me ill with jealousy seeing you with her. How would I get over that in Isabella's dream plan?"

"And I'm going to have to try very hard not to smash Jaime's face in when I see him next!"

"Fred, you're joking!"

"More or less, but you're right, I can't see us in an 'open marriage'."

"Sounds awful."

"Awful!" Noah laughed again and kicked his legs, practising his new vocal prowess and clearly requesting another raspberry.

Margot obliged.

Chapter Thirty-five

In the end, Emma didn't come back to San Pere. Her party had been really cool, and the next day, while they were still recovering, they were told they were needed for lots more promotional interviews. Linda was over the moon, as was Karl. Mikela and Chloe weren't so sure. Chloe didn't like the fuss, but then again it pleased her sponsors. Mikela just said no. She couldn't afford more time away from the restaurant, she would lose the job she loved. Emma was torn. She wanted to get back to Noah and Fred, but they were fine without her and once term started again, she would be stuck with them both full time. She didn't mean stuck, but still. Anyway, they needed her if Mikela wasn't going to be around.

"If it helps, we're going shopping this afternoon, we're going to glam you all up." The production company marketing guy was persuasive. After months of sweaty cycling gear, even after a bit of sea and sand, the idea of pampering and high heels was very seductive.

"Can't wait to see you all glamorous!" Karl winked at them all and then again at Emma. "That's the great thing with sportswomen, they look gorgeous in anything, no need to worry about dodgy camera angles or anything." Karl knew how to talk to them.

Emma let Fred know with a quick text, his reply was brief and unsurprised. The interviews were set up really quickly and the pace was hectic, but Emma loved it.

Fred and Margot took one day at a time. It felt like it was the only thing they could do. They tried to behave like they had at the beginning of the summer, but none of their extended family were fooled. None of them wanted to mention it either. One day at a time seemed to suit them all.

But then the final day came and it was time to head north. They had prepared and packed in advance, not wanting to spoil the last day. Lucie was heart-broken. She had to leave her beautiful Manté. Antonio had gone back to Madrid three days earlier, promising to write. She was happily heartbroken though. The summer had been the best, she was better and now they were all going home together. She was relieved not to have brought her old Barbie with her because she feared it might have met with a nasty end. It was so obvious that her mum and dad wanted to be together again, but there was still the massive obstacle of The Slut. If only she would go away and not come back this time. She'd make it up to Noah, so would her mum, he wouldn't miss out. At least going home meant that she would see Marigold, although she was pretty sure their neighbour would have adopted her completely by now.

Theo grabbed his dad in a massive hug to say goodbye. He whispered in his ear, "Sort it out, Dad. Really." Fred hugged him back and nodded with a kind of hopelessness, lifting his eyebrows as though there was nothing he could do. "No excuses, old man!"

Fred laughed and let his son go, slapping him on the back.

"Less of the old. See you in October, son, don't forget to do a bit of work!"

"Ha! I will if you will, Dad."

Uncle J had a tear in his eye as he prepared to wave them

off. Isabella had left again a couple of days before and the house was going to be very empty. As he hugged Margot, she held him by the arms and looked at him squarely.

"Get in the car and go and see her. Your time to be together is now. Tell her. You don't need to keep each other hanging any more."

Julian smiled wryly, "You're giving me relationship advice, young lady? But you could be right. Who needs an empty house at my age?"

"We'll be back in October."

Everybody was there for the final wave off. They waved as long as they could from the car and sighed with relief at the drop in emotion as they turned out of sight.

"I think we're going to have to sort of try Isabella's idea, Margot."

"You're kidding?" Margot was driving, but she was so surprised that she turned and looked directly at him.

"Well, it's that or empty houses, like J said."

"What the hell are you thinking?"

"Mu…" Lucie nearly interrupted to complain about language, but she didn't want to remind them that she could hear.

"Let's just tempt fate a little." Fred's expression was serious. "I'll suggest that Emma, Noah and I move back in with you, into Theo's room. Take it from there."

"Would she? Would we be OK with that?"

"Well, we would save on rent, have a garden, built in baby-sitters. She could go off on weekends whenever she wanted."

"And Noah and Dad would be there all the time, Mum!" Lucie couldn't contain herself, it was unhoped for. She felt her heart glue itself together a bit.

"So we kind of carry on like when we were on holiday? What about the neighbours?"

"Oh, Mum, who cares? Think about Noah."

Margot shook her head; she couldn't believe it. Even romantic little Lucie thought it was OK. "You'll kill me, the lot of you!"

Fred and Lucie took that as agreement and exchanged a high five. Fred squeezed Margot's knee. "It's the only way forward, anything else is too sad to contemplate."

Margot raised an eyebrow and was relieved to have a complicated bit of traffic to negotiate. It was a long drive home, she would have time to think.

Chapter Thirty-six

Emma got home after Fred. Noah was already asleep in bed. She kissed Fred briefly and rushed over to Noah's cot. She loved him so much when he slept.

"Did you have a good time? Lucie showed me some of the stuff you've been doing on Instagram and YouTube."

"It was great, really good fun. I can't wait to go out climbing though, I've missed it. Shall we go tomorrow?"

"No baby-sitter I'm afraid."

Emma's face fell, she'd forgotten again. Fred saw his chance.

"Actually Emma, what do you think of this as a plan?" He explained, opening a bottle of wine as he did so, not looking at her too closely. The wine bottle was half empty by the time he'd finished.

"It's true, this place has been empty all summer, while we've been paying rent. And I am going to have a lot more promo for the film to do. I was thinking of re-negotiating my contract to work a bit less anyway. With your plan, we can afford it." She smiled involuntarily, as she remembered Karl's sardonic expressions when he was explaining just how often there may be indispensable weekends away. "After all, it worked in Spain, why not?" She was also looking forward to the shocked expression on Bernie's face when he heard, let alone those of all the other staid old colleagues.

"Well, obviously, Margot has the last word, but I'll check

with her and ring the landlady in the morning. She can probably find someone straight away at this time of year."

The next weekend a noisy blackbird woke Margot up and she pinched herself. What had she agreed to? Her husband's mistress was going to move in with them. Poor Rufus, he really didn't like her, but he adored Fred and the baby. She could sympathise, she thought grimly. Anyway, if it didn't work, it didn't work.

Fred hadn't really thought through the details of how daily life would be. He hadn't imagined meals or chores, he had just wanted, with all his might, to leap first and face the obstacles after. Luckily there was Noah. He was over-excited by the move and the Saturday evening meal of take-away pizzas suited him fine. Having finished his organic baby food, he was banging his spoon, chortling and throwing pizza crusts at a delighted Rufus. Rufus was actually lying on his back next to the high chair, catching them. Lucie was thrilled to have her baby brother there. The three adults found that the pizzas had made them very thirsty for the nice red wine which Fred had bought earlier. They managed to keep things casual.

"I'm going climbing tomorrow, Fred, do you want to come?" Emma took another mouthful of wine.

"Not tomorrow, I don't think. I need to sort Noah out."

Margot breathed out, she couldn't believe that Emma had presumed she would babysit automatically like that, on the very first day. She had to trust Fred. Margot's room had an en-suite bathroom and they had decided that Lucie would use that and leave the main bathroom to Fred and Emma. This meant that at least they could all go to bed in a civilised manner.

The next morning Emma had got up and left early. When Fred came downstairs with Noah in his arms, Margot was emptying the cafetière. It was so familiar, in his own kitchen. He put his arms round her waist and turned her round. He kissed her lightly, she relaxed and they both kissed a squirming Noah.

"We did it!"

"But what have we done? I'll be cooking and cleaning and she'll be eating and having sex! "

"Not much of that any more I can tell you. Be patient. One day at a time." He kissed her again with promise and intent, until Noah hit him on the head.

Margot had friends whose older children had continued living at home with boyfriends or girlfriends and she couldn't help remembering their tales of annoying, egotistical behaviour. She bit her lip and put up with it. Fortunately, Fred was doing as much as he possibly could domestically and he had also asked Lucie to help out. Having a baby around, as well as two extra adults, made for a lot of extra washing and shopping, but they managed. Emma did contribute to some extent, but only on her terms.

They were into October when Margot realised that Emma was systematically gone at the weekend. She was so relieved when she left that she hadn't noticed how regular it had become. At first, she left on Friday afternoons, but now it was Thursday evenings. One Saturday afternoon, Fred was cutting the lawn, Margot was tidying up the flower beds and Lucie was playing with Noah on the part of the grass already mown, when Jan turned up unexpectedly.

"Hi, just passing by! Haven't seen you in ages. Oh Fred, you're here too, helping with the garden? That's good of you." Fred and Margot exchanged a look. Neither of them had been particularly forthcoming about their living arrangements with their friends so far. Margot's mother had shrugged and gone away for a couple of months which may or may not have been related. Fred's parents were still in blissful ignorance.

"Coffee? Beer? What do you fancy, Jan? Come and help me get it." Margot was flustered. Jan took the hint and followed her in the back door.

"What? I want is to know what's going on?" Jan was standing looking stern with her arms folded. "Are you back together? Have you been avoiding me?"

"Well, no and yes. I'll explain."

As she expected Jan was horrified, she couldn't accept that it was a justifiable situation.

"But I love Noah, you know we are all hard-wired to love dependant beings we look after and Fred and I, well... it's just the way it is."

"Can't he just chuck her out? Where is she now anyway?" Jan was simmering with the injustice of it all.

"We're taking it one day at a time and looking after ourselves to the best of our ability, it's called damage control. Come and see Lucie and Noah and you'll start to understand." Jan shook her head in disbelief and picked up the mugs to follow Margot outside. Then she found herself unwillingly participating, acting, as they all were, as if it was all perfectly normal. She couldn't help but admit that Noah was an adorable distraction. As she drove off, she was still reeling with the unfairness of it all. What might have been a source of titillating gossip, was simply sad.

That evening Lucie was staying with a friend, she wasn't inviting people back to the house for the moment by tacit agreement. This left Margot and Fred on their own, they bathed the baby and put him to bed, had a drink, cooked together, chatted amicably over their food and just felt wonderfully relaxed and normal. They took their last glass of wine to the sofa and Margot sank comfortably into the comfort of Fred's arms.

"How do you feel, Fred? Sorry to ask, I know Isabella would advise against it! But do you feel guilty?"

"I feel guilty all the time, but not towards Emma, hardly at all. I still feel horribly guilty to you and the kids. This feels right, here and now. This is what I want." They kissed and held each other tight, but then Margot pushed him away.

"I don't want to sleep with you, well I do, but not like this, like teenagers while the parents are away. I couldn't bear her looking at me knowingly as though she knew I had had the scraps and been grateful for them, while she had the three-course meal."

Fred laughed, "She hasn't had a three-course meal for a while, not with me anyway!"

"Well, that's another thing, I am a nurse after all…"

"OK, OK I get it. One day at a time, we can wait. Can I just woo you a little more now, please?" Fred didn't wait for an answer and kissed her again. An image of Julian and Isabella kissing under the shady tree flitted through his mind, making his lips curl in a smile, mid-kiss.

"What's so funny?" Margot was still a little on her guard.

"It's old Uncle J, some of his theories are spot on, kissing is under-rated." Margot smiled and relaxed and kissed him again.

Chapter Thirty-seven

Emma was staying with Linda again. As much as Linda loved her friend, she was busy with her job and, in fact, in a fledgling relationship with a fellow teacher. Emma had almost stopped asking if she could stay and was just turning up on Thursday night as though it was a given that the sofa would be hers. Often, she didn't leave until early Monday morning. Added to that, Linda had a heavy day on Fridays, it all became too much, she had had enough.

"Emma, you can't come every weekend. Don't you want to spend some time with Fred?"

"Not really. It's so boring. He always makes a fuss about Noah's bedtime or he wants to cut the lawn or walk the dog. Or he wants me to babysit while he trains with Bernie."

"Is it called baby-sitting when it's your baby?"

"You know what I mean."

"Are you seeing Karl this weekend?"

"Karl? Why?"

"Emma, this is me you're talking to. Why don't you finish with Fred if you want to be with Karl?"

"I don't, he doesn't, it's just… and there's Noah, Fred's his dad."

"I agree it's a mess, but you're going to have to do something, this place is not big enough for both of us, even if you paid me rent."

Emma felt like she'd been slapped. She had really, with a

reality check. She needed to decide what to do. She had thought she would have the upper hand with Margot as she was the one sleeping with Fred, but in fact she felt like a useless au-pair. The sort everyone makes jokes about. On top of that, Fred was really inhibited sexually in his son's old room with his ex and teenage daughter two doors away. Anyway, she wasn't that interested any more, she needed someone more like herself. Freer.

"I'm sorry, Linda, you're right. I've been taking advantage. I need to make some changes."

"You do… Actually tomorrow, for the awards ceremony for the film, I want to take Ethan, can you find somewhere else to crash?"

"Ah, is it getting serious with you two?" Emma was relieved to change the subject.

"Maybe, it feels right and it feels like the right time."

"My god, Linda, even you!"

"Yep! Even me!"

The next night was glossy and fun. They even won a prize for best image, success was in the air. Emma had asked Karl to book her a hotel room on expenses and he had agreed readily. As the last people left, Karl appeared at Emma's side.

"Share a taxi, Em? I'm in the same hotel."

So they did.

Emma normally hated Monday evenings. She got home before Fred as he had an after-school class. But this Monday she picked Noah up from the childminder they had found and gave him a big kiss before strapping him in his seat. He smiled at her with surprise. She didn't always kiss him like that.

"We're going to have to sort things out No-No. Mummy has some big stuff going on." Noah just smiled back, happy to hear her sounding cheerful for once.

Emma needed to speak to Fred on his own, but she was also desperate for a beer and some food and Noah needed feeding too. This meant that Emma was in full possession of the kitchen when Margot and Lucie got back.

"Hello, did you have a good weekend all of you? Noah seems in good form." Emma was determinedly friendly. "Will you join me for a beer, Margot?"

"I must grab a shower, first, I'll have one in a bit maybe." The last thing Margot wanted to do was drink beer while watching Emma making a mess in her kitchen. She'd been gone for four nights and the rest of them had morphed back into a normal family in that time, the contrast was stark. Lucie took herself off to watch Netflix, having given Noah and Rufus both a big hug. So Emma was alone with Noah when Fred got back. He walked through the door looking cheerful and relaxed, but as soon as he caught sight of her, his smile slipped and his expression became guarded.

"Hey." He kissed her briefly.

"Guess what?" Fred shrugged. "It's amazing news, I've been offered a fantastic job as a presenter on this new programme. It's being made by the same team who filmed us. It's been so successful that they've been backed by M6. It's a sort of competition, the contestants have to make their way from the south of Portugal to Athens using only manpower, you know the sort of thing, no money and plenty of challenges. Research starts next month and filming in February. It's honestly my dream job! I gave in my notice today. I can't wait!"

"You gave in your notice today, without telling me first, but I saw you at lunchtime."

"Come on, Fred, be honest, this is the perfect solution for

you. You look after Noah so much better than me anyway. Margot is here too. I will always be his mummy, but you are the proper parent. Stability is not for me. We never made any promises, did we? You knew this was never my forever plan."

Fred was taken aback, he wanted to defend Noah and being a parent, ask why she hadn't thought about all that before, defend himself even, but there was no point. He sat down heavily, her last sentence ringing in his ears.

"So just to be clear, you are splitting up with me?

"Be honest, Fred, it's already over, I don't see you weeping and wailing." Emma sat down opposite him.

Fred sat back and let out the breath he hadn't realise he'd been holding.

"Is there any more beer?"

Just then Margot came back downstairs, feeling stronger and refreshed. Emma passed them both a beer and explained again. She was bubbling with excitement, she'd already moved on in her head. Carefully maintaining neutral expressions, Fred and Margot shakily raised their bottles to toast Emma's new job, her future and ultimately theirs.

"Carpe diem!" Margot suggested as they clinked bottles. Noah raised his soggy biscuit in imitation and finally they all laughed.